W9-CEK-291

The Summer of Stuff

Carolyn Bradley

To the Wallingford Library
Enjoy! Carolyn Bradley

ISBN-13: 978-0692228012
ISBN-10: 0692228012

For my grandparents

CONTENTS

CHAPTER ONE

"You ready?"

He nodded slowly and wrapped his hand around the handle of the water gun, with one finger poised on the trigger.

I saw Robyn swim away from the pool stairs with the bright blue boat. The boat, contained the two floatie-hugging toddlers, Joshy and Lexie, and was just one of Robyn's many advantages in the battle. Audrey stood still in the dark night, our last rival guarding the stairs. She sighed and flopped down after checking to see if it was all clear; an easy victim.

The pool's underwater lights were blurred by Carter's quick kicks to stay afloat. He winked at me and took a deep breath before sinking into the illuminated water. His air bubbles moved across the pool and left a path for me to follow.

I waded in the water for a moment before following,

gripping the nozzle of my water gun with both hands. My short legs moved slowly through the pool and made small, unnoticeable ripples.

My heart pounded from the adrenalin building up and the coldness of the water. The whiff of air from the summer breeze formed small goose bumps along my arms. I bit my ice cold lips and sank down to attack with Carter.

"Fire!" Carter shouted as he popped up. Audrey shrieked and fell backwards onto the stairs. Carter got in a few good rounds of water blasts before Audrey could get back on her feet.

"You're horrible!" She screamed and filled up her water gun.

"Now, Allison!" Carter poked me with his foot. Chlorine from the pool water blurred my vision and fueled my desire to win.

Multiple rounds were shot from both sides making it difficult to tell where the stairs were. Audrey knew that this would be her downfall, but there was nothing for her to do except fight back.

"Enough! It's not fair! Two against one! Not fair!" Audrey moaned. I gripped the top my water gun and lowered it down, waiting for Audrey to forfeit.

"So you'll give up?" I smirked and refilled my water gun while she rested.

"Never," she breathed.

"I thought you would say that," Carter smiled deviously, and the fighting continued.

"Robyn! Help! They are taking control of the stairs!" Audrey shouted, squirting her gun as fast as she could.

Her water ammo was low and if she stopped, she would have to give up.

Robyn couldn't leave Lexie and Joshy alone. Both babies to the game they'd soon be part of, Lexie and Joshy were simply too young to swim without supervision.

"Just give them the stairs!" called Robyn from the opposite side of the pool. "We'll reclaim it when we're ready!" Carter grunted at the thought of them reclaiming anything we worked so hard for.

"Fine," Audrey muttered as she dove into the water. She kicked hard, splashing big waves in our faces.

"Yes! We did it! Allison! Finally! The long wait! The plans have finally worked!" Carter danced on the stairs, shouting with excitement.

"Now all we'll have to do is keep the stairs," I whispered loud enough for Carter to hear over the beat of his own enthusiastic heart. He nodded slightly, but continued acting like the child he was. I didn't blame him though. He'd been so distraught ever since we lost the stairs in the battles last year to Robyn and Audrey. He had been planning our revenge ever since.

As we laughed and sat on the stairs, I felt Robyn's eyes on me. Glaring, her big green eyes spotted me and singled me out. I could feel her trying to get inside of us; reading our lips as we spoke to each other.

"Okay how about this? One of us stays at the stairs and the other attacks. Then we switch off. See?" Carter calculated.

"Yeah, maybe. But, what if Audrey or Robyn, or both, come to attack?" I asked back.

"Then whoever is attacking sneaks up behind them and fires. That way they couldn't attack, because they'd be cornered. The defense just has to call for help. The offense would need to take over the boat first though…if no one was guarding." Carter started rambling again. "The defense would need to hold them off for a while, I guess and -"

"Okay, I get it!" I laughed and rolled my eyes. Carter smirked and filled up his water gun quickly.

"Sorry," he grinned. "Who should go first?"

"You go first. I'll guard the stairs," I told him. Carter nodded and started out to the boat. I saw his little head vanish under the hazy water, and then pop up again, a couple feet from where I stood.

Lexie and Joshy were just climbing out of the rubber boat to play in the grass, creating a perfect time to steal it away without anyone noticing.

"Grab it! Grab it and run!" I yelled to Carter. Robyn flinched at the sound of my voice and saw Carter's little hand grab their boat.

"Audrey! Get our boat!" Robyn called in desperation. "Save it! Save it!"

There was nothing for me or Robyn to do. It was up to our teammates to win this for us. I thought about helping, but this was Carter's heroic moment.

Carter knew his sister's weaknesses, and in that moment her biggest weakness was feet. Audrey was literally afraid of feet and she had been ever since Carter got warts in kindergarten. Just one touch of someone else's foot against her skin, would make her want to throw up.

"Get your warty toes away from me!" Audrey shrieked. Carter had won.

"Carter! Yes! We are the champions! The winners! Carter, you did it!" I cried with elation. I saw Carter's bright red face lift from the water, a full smile stretched from cheek to cheek. "Too much swimming?"

"No," he huffed. He wanted to seem strong, but his quickening breath said otherwise.

"You were awesome, even if you're a little tired," I smiled, pulling the boat close to our newly claimed stairs.

"Thanks," he breathed heavily, floating over the deepest stair. His cherry red face slowly glowed back to his normal tan appearance.

"So is this battle thing over now?" I asked Carter as the twilight sky turned to a dark gray. The stars seemed to cheer for us, sparkling with congratulations.

"Allison, you know that this is never over. We just won a battle of this never-ending war," Carter laughed. He looked to the sky, bobbing in the water, and I couldn't help but laugh along with him because I knew he was right. The battle had been going on for years before that summer, and no one wanted it to end.

In the early weeks of July, my sisters and I would travel to our grandparents' house where we'd spend the rest of summer while our parents worked back home. Audrey, Carter, and Joshy would wait in their house next door until we drove up in Grandma's old van from the airport. As we jumped out of the car, they'd always run over and say the same thing.

"Where have you been all year? Ready for summer?"

CHAPTER TWO

"Grandma?" asked towel-wrapped Lexie.

"Yes dear?" Grandma smiled down at little Lexie who would be turning four next spring.

"Why do we have to say goodbye to Audrey, Carter, and Joshy?" Grandma just chuckled and squeezed Lexie's tiny soft hand.

"We have to say goodbye because we have to go to bed. They have to go to bed too, Lexie. It's rather late," Grandma whispered picking her up in her arms. Aunt Stella strolled up behind to jump in the conversation.

"And," she added, "we can always see them again tomorrow." Aunt Stella smiled and went to catch up with Robyn, leaving me tagging from behind. We only had to walk a short distance to get to Grandma's house. As we ventured up the stairs to the front door, I saw Grandpa sitting in his chair doing his favorite activity, reading.

"Where were you? I was worried," Grandpa

grumbled as we enter through the main door. Grandma snorted. With a book in his hand and his drink half full, it was hard to believe that he was worried at all.

"Of course you were, Grandpa," Grandma mumbled and made her way through the living room to the kitchen.

"Do you need any help Grandma?" Robyn asked, still in her swimsuit and towel.

"No, no dear. You go. Get ready for bed," Grandma urged Robyn to the stairs.

"But Grandma…" Robyn slumped up into the room she shared with me. "I really can help," Robyn persisted.

"I know you can, but have you seen the time? Why, it's almost 10:30!"

"It's summer too, Grandma. We can stay up late in the summer!" Robyn called from our room.

"Grandma?" I whispered as she stumbled back over to the sink.

"No, you can't help either," she said without taking her eyes off of the plate in her hand. She hurried through two more before I could say anything else.

"I wasn't asking that," I tried to explain. "I was going to ask if I could take a shower."

"Lexie is just about done. Go head upstairs."

Trudging up the stairs, I heard little Lexie singing "Mary Had a Little Lamb" from the tub. Aunt Stella was in the hall, leaning on the bathroom door.

"You almost done in there, Lexie? Do you need any help?" Aunt Stella asked when Lexie stopped singing in the middle of the song. "Lexie?" Aunt Stella was just about to knock when Lexie, bound up in a bright pink towel, opened the door.

"See? I'm a big girl. I can do it all by myself," Lexie said, hugging the towel to her wet skin.

"How did you wash your hair, silly girl?" Aunt Stella asked, pointing at Lexie's messy, bubbly hair.

"With soap, of course," Lexie mumbled. Her baby curls stuck out in odd places and her adorable frown looked out of place next to her red cheeks. My aunt giggled and played with Lexie's hair.

"You need some help. Get back in the bath tub," Aunt Stella said, turning Lexie around.

"Wait! I need to shower. Grandma said I could," I objected.

"Allison, Lexie needs to get all of this soap out of her hair before you can shower. Maybe in the morning? You should shower then."

I plodded into the bedroom, angry and frustrated, but in no mood to argue. Everyone seemed to be doing something and getting stuff done, while I was sent to bed.

"Grandma didn't let you help clean either?" Robyn asked me as I crawled under my covers. Robyn slept on the top bunk, I slept on the bottom.

"Nah, I just wanted to take a shower. Lexie's in there, so I'd have to wait for a long time," I complained.

"Whatever," Robyn moaned and rolled over.

****

"Morning girls!" Grandma called, waking me from a deep sleep. Robyn and I rubbed our eyes and dragged ourselves down the seemingly long stairs. "How did you all sleep?"

"Fine," Robyn grumbled. "Just perfect."

"What do you both want for breakfast? We have toast, five kinds of cereal, oatmeal, bagels, English muffins, frozen waffles – "

"Oatmeal!" I interrupted, pointing at my braces. I got them on about a week before I came. I didn't want to break them by eating anything hard so soon.

"Right." Grandma pulled out her notepad. "One order of oatmeal. How about you Robyn? Oatmeal too?"

"Ew! I hate oatmeal. I'll just have some Cheerios."

Grandma scribbled down our orders while we took our seats at the small, round table.

"Umph," Grandpa mumbled as he took his seat at the front of the table.

"What'll you have, Grandpa?" Grandma asked in the sweetest of voices.

"Glass of water and my pills, please," Grandpa answered back, definitely in his good-morning mood.

"That is all you want for breakfast? No food?"

"Well, maybe some oatmeal," Grandpa smiled.

"Alrighty. Two orders of oatmeal and one of Cheerios. Got it." Grandma poured two packets of oatmeal into two bowls and poured some hot water on each. "Aunt Stella! Breakfast!"

"Let her sleep. She is in another performance this afternoon," Grandpa yawned.

"Another? She's just wearing herself down," Grandma sighed, handing me and Grandpa our bowls of strawberry oatmeal. I ran my tongue over my braces and grabbed a spoon.

"I've been trying to tell her that. She just won't

listen," Grandpa complained.

"Here," Grandma handed Robyn her bowl of cereal. "I'm going to the store today. Need anything?"

"Nope," I gulped down my oatmeal.

"I don't," Robyn said.

"Uh, maybe some soap for the upstairs bathroom… and some duct tape to fix that hole… Oh! And some more fertilizer," Grandpa added.

"Got it," Grandma sighed. "Are you planning to go out and pull some weeds with Grandpa today?"

"No," Robyn said flatly.

"Well," I said in return, looking at Robyn. "I am. I'd love to spend some time outside." Robyn grunted and slurped the last sips of milk from her bowl.

"I might," Robyn mumbled, shooting me a look. "Maybe."

"Great! I'll buy some more of those gardening tools. Kids' size," Grandma smiled, but her eyes darted across the window that framed us from behind. "Oh! Did you see that little robin?" She pointed to the window, displaying a red and brown bird on the feeder. "He was nibbling at the bird feeder! How exciting! Do you see him?"

"I see him too, but I won't see him for long if you keep startling him," Grandpa interrupted her, starring at the beautiful red bird.

"Oh, sorry." Grandma sat down at the table, shaking her head, "it's just that those little birds always make me so excited. Allison, you'll need to write about this nature moment in your diary." Robyn let out a hard, forced giggle.

"It's not my diary," I explained. "It's like a news report on everything that happens while I'm here. That way I can write about it, every little detail, when I get home. I'm hoping to write a novel someday."

"Tish!" Grandpa yelled in my ear. "You're too young to write a novel. Novels are long and well written, by adults."

"I can write a novel."

"Prove it," Robyn snickered.

"Alright, I will," I protested sadly, "when I get home."

"Ha!" Robyn started.

"Stop it. You are making her upset. She can dream. It's good to have dreams," Grandma whispered taking a sip of tea.

"Not dreams like that. Dreams like getting A's on a report card are good dreams for young kids. My dream was to go to space. Did that ever happen? No. No it didn't. But I got close. I worked for NASA for 30 years! That's pretty impressive, huh? I'd hate to see you upset if it didn't work out," Grandpa snorted. "I'd find a realistic goal, if I were you."

My eyes started to tear up; I was done being pestered by my own family.

"Come on, Allison! Grandpa was just kidding!" Grandma yelled as I climbed the stairs to my room. *Knock, Knock, Knock.*

"Oh, Audrey and Carter. Robyn is in the kitchen. Allison is upstairs," Grandma answered the door.

"Guys! Let's go! We're going on the trampoline! Wanna come?" Carter yelled as he wiped his muddy sneakers on the welcome rug.

"Sure!" Robyn called from the kitchen.

"Allison? You coming?" Audrey looked up the stairs. I glanced down, seeing everyone huddled around the stairs, waiting for my answer.

"Sure. Why not?" I put my mind in a better mood, not trying to think about what happened in the kitchen.

"Hey, I'll race you!" Carter nudged me as I reached the last couple stairs.

"Bring it," I smirked back.

"Ready... Set..."

"Wait! Let me get my shoes on first!" I hollered. I slipped my old Converse sneakers on, tied them up slowly, loving the anxious look on Carter's face. "Okay, I'm ready."

"GO!" Carter shouted, ignoring the disapproving, irritated look from my Grandma. We raced all the way back to Carter's house. We jump the unfinished, rugged fence to the backyard and continue running until we reached the trampoline. I touch it first, but Carter claimed he'd won the race.

"Robyn! You saw didn't you? I got here before Allison, right?" Carter objected.

"Yeah, sure, whatever... Let's just jump! Can we play 'Wolf'? Or 'Hot Potato'? Audrey, please?" Robyn asked our leader in trampoline games.

"We need to get on the trampoline first guys." Audrey stuck her hands out on the trampoline and swiftly pulled herself on top.

Audrey chose the first game, a game that Carter could barely stand.

"We're going to play, 'Wish!' game. Okay?" Audrey said. Carter stood, a frown on his face, obviously upset.

"Do we have to? Why can't we play 'Chicken' or 'Monkey in the Middle'?" Carter whined.

"I always get to pick first. That's just the way it is. Audrey first," Audrey stuck her head high in the air and fluffed her strawberry blonde locks.

"Fine. I chose next," Carter moaned.

CHAPTER THREE

"Robyn! You first." Audrey pointed her long finger at Robyn.

"Why can't I go first?" Carter complained. "You're so bossy."

"Am not," Audrey stated and raised her eyebrows. "Go Robyn. Before Carter takes our whole day away, complaining."

"Seriously, I don't complain very much. I only complain when you are around." Carter reminded Audrey.

"Well, here I go." Robyn sat herself down on the trampoline. Carter, Audrey, and I joined her, making a pear-like shape around the edge of the trampoline. "I wish that I would get chocolate for dinner! Okay, everyone do the chant!" We all jumped up and started singing and jumping around Robyn, who was still seated on the trampoline.

We started the chant in a deep low voice and slowly got higher as our bounces got more aggressive.

"I wish! I wish!" We sang the song that had become so ingrained in our friendship that it felt like summer had finally started.. "I wish that we'd get chocolate for dinner! I wish that we'd get chocolate for dinner!" Carter, Audrey, and I yelled and sang at the top of our lungs. That was the fun of it, yelling and screaming. "Robyn! Robyn! Your wish will come true! Your wish will come true!" We all fell down on our backs and continued the routine cheer. "Bounce us like popcorn! Jump us like frogs!" Robyn had to jump and get us off the ground. Carter was easy. Audrey was even easier. I wanted to hold still like a rock, and never let her bounce me. In the game, if she got everyone to bounce up in the air once, her wish would come true. I held my ground for a long time, staying wrapped tightly in fetal position, so Robyn was out of breath when she finally put me in the air.

"Ha! Got you," she breathed. "Since I bounced Carter first, he gets to be next." Carter smiled. Audrey frowned and crossed her arms.

"I wish that Audrey was younger than I am right this very minute so I can be bossy to her instead of her being bossy to me!"

"Carter, that's too long." Audrey rolled her eyes.

"Sorry. I'll try again." Carter winked and cleared his throat, hardly disturbed by Audrey's endless mocking. "I wish that I was older than Audrey! Good?"

"Perfect," I nodded and stood up to sing. Audrey frowned.

"What is it Audrey? Is something wrong?"

"Yeah, I don't get it," Audrey crossed her arms and sat down, crisscross-apple-sauce.

"What don't you get?" I asked her.

"I don't get why I have to say something about myself," Audrey pouted. "I refuse to say his wish." After much disagreeing and arguing, Carter decided to skip his turn.

"Brat," he mumbled as he sat down, eyeing the now content Audrey. "Allison, you're turn."

"Me?" I ask pointing to myself. "What about you Audrey?"

"Nah, I don't want to go after Carter," Audrey glanced snottily at Carter, rolled her eyes, and continued. "Besides, best for last!"

"Well, okay." I sat myself up and brushed away the thick strands of hair that stuck to my cheeks. "I wish. I wish-"

"No! No! No, no, no!" Audrey flailed her arms in the air. "Stop!" She snapped.

"What? What did I do?" I asked franticly.

"Audrey doesn't like it when you don't have enough enthusiasm," Carter leaned over and whispered to me.

"Allison!" Audrey whined. "Don't ruin the fun. Holler it!"

"Got it," I took in a deep breath and began again with ten times more enthusiasm. "I wish! I wish! I wish that I could write a book!"

"Allison, why do you want to write a book?" Carter interrupted my chant. Audrey rolled her eyes, annoyed that Carter was making her beloved game so difficult to get through.

"It's her dream," Robyn mocked me. "Ouch! I'm only telling the truth." She continued after receiving a strong punch in the arm. "You want to write a book. No need for violence." Robyn rubbed her arm in fake pain.

"Excuse Robyn's comment," I said. "I want to write a book because I love to write. That's it. Writing is my favorite thing to do. Oh! That reminds me!" I pulled out a small notebook from my back pocket, the kind of notebook that Grandma used to take our meal orders. I flipped to the first page and start scribbling down some notes.

"What're you doing?" Audrey asked, her green eyes peering over my shoulder.

"Taking notes," I answered, still hurriedly writing. Writing things down had been a passion of mine after realizing I wasn't too good at taking pictures to remember a moment.

"Why?" Carter asked, his small face perks up.

"Because," I shrugged. "If I take notes, then I'll have lots of material to put in my book. Of course I'm going to have to write a book about summer. I mean, there's just so much to remember." Robyn yawned.

"Let's go to the treehouse," she suggested. "I'm getting bored."

"Okay," I said. "Just let me finish one more note." As I looked up, content with my notes thus far, Carter, Audrey, and Robyn were already racing towards the big oak tree in the back of the Audrey and Carter's backyard. "Wait for me! Hey? Guys!" I jumped in the race, gaining speed and soon catching up to Audrey, then Robyn. I was neck-in-neck with Carter, soon speeding ahead, but then falling back after I realized that I was out of breath.

"Ha! Allison, you're fast, but not fast enough to beat- THE CARTERMAN!" Carter proudly declared.

"The Carterman? Best you could come up with?" I laughed, taking breaths between each word.

"It's a work in progress. Kinda like your book." I followed him up the ladder to our treehouse. Like most of the things we start in summer, the treehouse was a work in progress too.

"Looky here! We need to sign our names again and date. Gotta keep it posted!" Carter pointed to the tree branch that held our inscribed names. We etched in our names every summer that we visited; starting before my sister Lexie was even born, but after Robyn and I were old enough to start flying as unaccompanied minors. We wrote our names that first summer only in marker, but as we grew older, we began to carve our names in the tree branch with knives – Swiss Army knives. We realized that the marker would wash off after a day, and we couldn't let our memories be lost after just one night of rain.

"Let's carve our names again!" Robyn shouted. We followed behind as she climbed the ladder to where the small treehouse was hidden behind bright green leaves. "We let this become a wreck. Spring cleaning in summer is what we need." Robyn took her hand and wiped the wall. "See, dirt." She said, showing us her hand covered in grime. The lines that made up her hand were black.

"Yuck! It smells like someone had a mud fight up here," Audrey plugged her nose as she came in. "What's that in the corner? Carter? Did you put that here?" All heads turned. Sitting in the corner of the treehouse was a little brown paper bag.

"I'm not gonna touch it. I don't know what's in there." Carter backed away.

"It's not like a disease is in there, Carter," Robyn was the brave one and peaked inside before sticking her dirty hand into the bag.

"What do you feel?" Audrey whispered.

All of a sudden Robyn yanked her arm out from the bag, and screamed in pain.

****

"Robyn! What is it? Are you okay?" I asked anxiously. "Where's the first aid?" By the time I finished panicking, Robyn had stopped yelling and started laughing.

"Robyn? You okay?" Carter's thick eyebrows formed one line of concern.

"Duh! I'm fine! Nothing bad is in that paper bag. Allison, no need to freak out. You sound like Mom." I slammed my hand against my heart, gasping for breath.

"Well," I gasped, "you didn't need to do that. You almost gave me a heart attack."

"I think she did give you a heart attack." Carter nudged me playfully. "What's in there anyway?"

"Aw, just some candy – it actually looks like it hasn't been here long at all," Robyn shrugged. "Nothing much."

"CANDY?" Carter asked excitedly. He started doing his happy dance, the same dance he performed when we won the water battle. "REALLY?"

"To be exact, four pieces," Audrey said examining the brown paper bag. "One for each of us."

"That's weird," Robyn said.

"It doesn't matter! It's candy! Let's eat!" We each took a piece of candy. I took the Snickers, Robyn took the Tootsie Roll, Audrey took the lollipop, and Carter took the king-size Hershey bar.

"Yum," Carter munched and licked his chocolate covered finger tips.

"Carter, you just gobbled that down. Have some manners," Audrey slapped Carter's arm, licking her cherry lollypop. "Girls never act like that."

"Speak for yourself," Robyn said, finishing her tootsie roll in one mouthful. "I wonder what we'll find tomorrow. I wanna know who put this here."

"I bet it's just a one-time thing. But, I'll take some notes, for my story of course."

"You know you'd need a problem," Carter mumbled licking his lips.

"A problem? For what?" Audrey asked.

"A problem for a story. You know, like a conflict. Allison, you'll need one. You're never going to have a good story if you don't have a problem that the characters in the story have to sort out."

"You're my problem now, Carter," I ruffled his blonde hair playfully.

"Did we carve our names? We still need to do that."

"Yeah!" Carter cheered. He pulled out his Swiss and began to carve his name. When he finished he handed the knife to Audrey. "Here, your turn. We have to go in

28

order, by age."

"Then Robyn goes next. I'm older." Audrey corrected proudly.

"Gosh. You make it seem like a big deal. You're just a little older. Like a month, seriously," Robyn carved her name and handed it back to Audrey.

"Ready, Allison? You have to put the date too." I gestured a thumbs up and took the little knife.

"I don't know where to sign. The branch is full." The branch was full of our signatures, dates, and doodles; full of memories of past summers.

"Sign here." Carter pointed to an open spot on the top. "We'll need to find another branch next year."

After I signed, I paused and ran my hand over the full branch. It felt bittersweet, but I smiled anyway and turned to my friends. Our original branch was full, but that didn't mean that our time together was over.

CHAPTER FOUR

"Can you believe we're going into sixth grade next year?" Audrey asked Robyn as we headed back to the trampoline. Lunch was coming and we had only played one trampoline game.

"Middle school. Finally," Robyn sighed.

"Yeah, well, it's not that awesome. Just more homework and new teachers. Like any other year," I told her.

"Uh, duh, it's totally awesome! You get lockers! You get to switch classes! You get your first kiss! It's so awesome!" Robyn exclaimed.

"Eww, kisses," Audrey muttered, interrupting Robyn. "It's just middle school."

"Yeah, it's no big deal. I haven't had my first kiss yet, and I'm in middle school," I explained.

"The only reason you haven't been kissed yet is because of your attitude about everything. You're always a downer." Robyn broke from her small daydream and back into reality.

"I'm not downing middle school, I'm just telling the truth."

"Still," Robyn turned her head, irritated. "Gosh, I'd be better off getting advice from Lexie."

"What games do you guys want to play?" Carter asked us when we finally got to the trampoline. He must have run ahead. Next school year, he'd be the only one not in middle school.

"Um, let's play 'Wolf,'" Audrey suggested. The premise of the game was to make the most noise to distract the wolf. Whoever is the wolf has to catch you to get you to be the next wolf.

"Audrey! I got you! I did!" Carter yelled during his turn being the wolf.

"Redo the play," I said.

"No! I got her! I know it!" Carter persisted.

"But I've been the wolf three times already!" Audrey whined.

"I'll be wolf! I haven't gone yet," Robyn suggested. Carter gave up and let Robyn go.

"Okay, go sit in the middle. We'll start." The rest of us began jumping around, screaming in hopes that we wouldn't be the next one caught.

"Are you hungry, Wolfie?" Carter mocked her. Robyn frowned and glared at him.
"You're going down, Carter," she mumbled. "But not until I get Allison."

"Grab her!" Audrey shouted as Robyn bounced up from her spot on the trampoline. She chased me around a few times, but soon I stopped running and gave her the satisfaction.

"Close your eyes, we'll start," Carter told me once I took my seat in the middle. I kept my eyes closed for most of the beginning, but I couldn't help but peek and giggle at their silly jumping.

That's when I saw them.

Two boys, who looked around my age, sat beneath a huge tree close to the trampoline.

"Guys! Stop!" I yelled, jumping up and almost knocking Audrey on the head. I bounced off the trampoline and approached the intruders. Audrey, Robyn, and Carter soon saw them too and decided to join me.

"Who are you guys? How long have you been here watching us?"

"Long enough for us to laugh a few times," the first boy said.

"What were you guys doing anyway?" The second boy asked.

"None of your business," Audrey snapped back. The two boys understood that they wouldn't be receiving an answer and smirked. "What's your name?" Audrey asked the first boy.

"I'm Rob. This is my brother Travis. We're twins."

"No kidding," Robyn muttered, eyeing the matching clothes. "What are you guys doing here?"

"Well, we heard some yelling and we thought someone was being murdered, so we decided to check it out," Travis replied smoothly.

"Why would you check out a murder?" Audrey looked confused.

"Sarcasm," Travis said.

"Weirdoes," Carter sighed. "We're trying to play a game. We don't need an audience."

"Can we play?" Travis asked. "We just moved in," Travis said pointing to the house next to Audrey and Carter's. "We have nothing to do all summer."

"You can't play," Audrey said sharply. Travis and Rob looked hurt, and I hated being mean.

"No, you guys should play. More is better," I encouraged. Instantly Rob and Travis's faces lit up, while Audrey, Robyn, and Carter's faces fell.

"Allison," Carter muttered, tugging on my arm. "I don't want them to play. Besides, you just came to visit! I don't want to ruin it."

"Don't be jealous, Carter," I laughed, but Carter scowled "We are going to let them play." I said firmly. "Summer is supposed to be fun and a time to make new friends. We never do that. Let's try." Carter sighed and nodded sadly.

"So what are your names anyway?" Rob called to us. He and Travis were already seated on the trampoline's edge, waiting for us. I could tell that Carter, Robyn, and Audrey were hesitant to answering Rob's question. So I took charge.

"My name is Allison. This is my sister Robyn, and my friends Carter and Audrey Fergus." I tell them, pointing to each of us. They nod, not paying any real attention to what I was explaining. Though I already got the vibe that they were jerks, I kept my mouth shut. I wasn't going to join in to all the negativity.

For some reason, Audrey was feeling more and more

irritated with the twins' presence. I could tell by the sudden redness in her cheeks and the way her eyes grew wider and then smaller in rapid repeats. Travis and Rob couldn't tell, because they hadn't known her long enough. This was the start of a horrible rivalry. Audrey vs. the New Boys.

"You guys ready to play?" Travis asked, slipping off his sneakers.

"No! I don't want to play!" Audrey busted out. "You guys intruded and interrupted our game! How dare you!"

"Where did you come from? Why did you come here?" Carter asked them, joining into Audrey's harshness.

They were obviously shocked by all the drama. There was a moment of silence, and I was able to get a real good look at each twin. They both had blue eyes, but slightly different color hair. Rob had light brown hair that stood straight up and Travis had dark brown hair that flopped down on his forehead.

"I thought new friends would be good. You guys seem like you woke up on the wrong side of the bed," Rob snarled, pointing at Audrey, Carter and Robyn. "But, you, you seem alright. Too bad the rest of you can't go for change. Let's go Travis, we can just Skype with our old friends." Rob gave us a dirty look, while Travis just looked really hurt. They hurried out of the yard without fully getting their shoes on.

"Guys! Why'd you do that?" I asked frustrated. Audrey looked away, ashamed of her method to get them to leave. An anger management class was calling her name.

"Hey! You never answered my question!" Carter shouted to Travis and Rob as they ran down the street. "Why did they move into the Marvinson's house? The Marvinson's didn't move away."

"Duh, Carter! Remember the Marvinson's coming over to Mom and Dad, asking for kid advice? Mrs. Marvinson never had any children, so they must have adopted Travis and Rob." Audrey hit her head in frustration. "I shouldn't have been so mean! I just can't help it sometimes."

"I told you," I said in my kindest, yet snarkiest tone. She looked away, upset. "We need to fix this." By the time we agreed to change our view on making friends, the twins were long gone, and our chances had vanished.

"I was just embarrassed. I wasn't trying to ignore them! I tried to talk to them but it never seemed to be a good time." Robyn sat down. "I'm just kind of shy, I guess."

We joined her on the trampoline and began to come up with ideas to make-up with Travis and Rob. We talked until we had a plan, it must have been a long time because before we realized it, we were called in for lunch.

"I'm having grilled cheese!" Carter smiled cheerfully, trying to forget what happened thirty minutes before.

"Yum," I said unenthusiastically. "The plan is settled, right?" I ask once more, to be sure that what we decide will be the final, last word.

"Yeah, sure," Robyn said, sounding uneasy and a little bit frightened about the whole situation.

"We'll do it after lunch, my house," Audrey told us

35

before running inside. Robyn and I raced back home and Grandma met us at the door.

"What'll you have for lunch today? Orders anyone?"

"I'll have Mac n' Cheese," Robyn said, taking the same seat at the kitchen table as that morning and the night before, "with emphasis on the cheese."

"Allison? What will you have?" Grandma asked me again. My mind was still full of uneasy thoughts of Travis and Rob. It made me sick how we treated them, and my stomach flipped with the thought of having to confront them again so soon. I stared up into Grandma's face.

"My head hurts. I don't want anything to eat."

"Don't you go start acting like Grandpa!" Grandma snapped. I was shocked at her response, but took it as a personal use of knowledge. Never act like Grandpa when Grandma is around.

"Sorry, I, uh, guess I'll have a cold slice of pizza. If that's alright," I told her, all I wanted to do was take a nap; a great, big, dreamy nap.

"Okay. I'll get those ready for you. Aunt Stella! Grandpa!" Aunt Stella solemnly entered the kitchen, mumbling to herself. "What's wrong honey?"

"I, I... Uh, stuff to do! Memorize lines!" Aunt Stella mumbled on.

"She has to take the part of Agnesse. The actress called in sick with a horrible flu, so Stella has to take her part, along with her own part in the show. Agnesse is a rather large part with many lines, I suppose, so she's been memorizing lines all morning. The show's tomorrow night. And we're going," Grandpa explained entering and sitting down gruffly. Aunt Stella moaned.

"Girls," Grandma said turning toward us, shifting her focus, "I've heard that there are some new kids in the neighborhood. Two boys, I think. The Marvinsons, bless their souls, have adopted two boys. Stella, take your seat sweetie."

"Have you girls met these boys?" Grandpa asked. Robyn and I glanced and caught each other's eyes. We were thinking the same thing. Lie, lie, lie.

"No we haven't Grandma," Robyn said plainly. "I'm sure we'd be the best of friends though." Lies, lies, lies.

"Good, that's so sweet." Grandma smiled and placed our lunch in front of us. "Lexie! Come here, sweetie!"

"She's downstairs playing with Joshy. I'd like to eat in peace. Don't call her up," Grandpa murmured taking a bite out of his usual sandwich, turkey with American cheese, one slice tomato and one piece of lettuce.

"Fine, but she'll be hungry later." Grandma sat down and took a bite out of her sandwich. "What are you doing after lunch?"

"Going to Audrey and Carter's," I said.

"Like always."

CHAPTER FIVE

"So with your mom baking cookies, that means we just have to pick the flowers and that will be that," Robyn said to Carter after we all finished our lunches.

"No, not exactly," Audrey answered back wearily. "We still need to go over to their house apologize and well, who knows what's next!"

"Guys, come on! It'll be fun to make new friends," I encouraged them.

"Whatever," Audrey mumbled. She looked away, angry at the thought of becoming friends with the enemy; her enemy.

"You never know, they could be really nice!" I said. "When I first met my best friend–"

"I know, I know," Robyn interrupted. "She was really irritating, but then you got to know her, blah, blah, blah." Carter giggled and ran up ahead.

"I bet I'll beat you guys there!" He yelled back at us.

"I bet so too!" Robyn yelled. She didn't feel like running, neither did Audrey or me. We didn't feel like picking flowers illegally from the Fergus's backyard.

"You know what?" Audrey spoke at random.

"What?" Robyn and I said in unison.

"If I get in trouble for trying to make friends, by picking my Mom's flowers, I'm blaming you," Audrey said, pointing at me.

"Why me? I'm just encouraging you, not forcing you," I told her promptly.

"Yeah, yeah. Strongly encouraging me," Audrey muttered. "Let's catch up to Carter, don't want him to take all the good flowers."

We ran up to meet Carter, who was busy under the hot summer sun. The sun blazed down rays on our tank-top covered backs. It felt good, like a warm happy feeling, but it also felt horrible, knowing that we were only out here because of our bad attitudes. Every so often we'd have to squat down, ducking from the sight of Mrs. Fergus. Mrs. Fergus was Audrey and Carter's mother, prize winner of babysitting and pie-baking. She's the All-American stay-home kind of mom. Loving and sweet, gentle and caring; except when it comes to her pansies and chrysanthemums. I bet that she loved those flowers more than her nearly ritualistic pie baking.

"Don't let her see you," Carter warned us. Right then, we could see her through the window, playing with one of our favorite little distractions, Joshy. "Tell me when you each have ten. We can keep them out here or behind our backs when we go get the cookies. In fact, I'll ask if they're done right now!" Carter jumped up and ran the back door.

"What is he doing? Giving away our flower picking spot?" Audrey babbled in spite. She cornered her patch of flowers and handed me some that she found on the ground.

"No," I whispered back. "He just wants to find out when the cookies will be ready."

"Now would be a great time to stop picking and run up the side of the house," Robyn said, focusing at Mrs. Fergus's departure from the window. "She's gone."

"You're right, let's go. I've got Carter's flowers." Audrey picked up the bouquet of Carter's flowers and ran to the side of the yellow house. Robyn and I followed her, quickly and quietly. After about a minute or two of heavy breathing against the cold wall, Carter came out holding a plate of cookies.

"I told her that we'd eat them out here while we're playing," Carter whispered. "Let's go before it's too much later." We hurried to the big green Marvinson house.

It looked scary as we approached it and I half-expected a monster to pop out of the window to tell us to run back home. None of us felt good about what we'd done, but none of us really liked apologizing either. *Ding, Dong*

"Hello?" Mrs. Marvinson answered the door. Looking down at our innocent faces, she smiled. "Oh, how sweet. Boys? I think some of the neighborhood children have brought you some welcome cookies!"

Travis and Rob approached the door, their faces grim at the sight of us. "Allison, Robyn, Audrey, Carter?

Have you met my boys? This is Travis, and this is Robby."

"Rob," Rob corrected.

"Right, Rob. Sorry," Mrs. Marvinson looked embarrassed, a bit rushed, and backed up a bit, pushing Rob and Travis closer to the door. "I'll let you children talk. I've, uh, left my iron on." Mrs. Marvinson hurried out of the room.

"What do you want?" Rob asked rudely. "Come to yell at us some more?"

"Hey! Listen here-" Audrey began.

"We just came to say we're sorry and want to be your friends." I quickly interrupted Audrey, nervous at what she could have said. I wasn't going to have her ruin this chance too.

"Yeah, right. Your mom probably sent you over here." Travis said.

"No, we came over by ourselves. We felt bad and wanted to make-up. Will you accept our offer?" I asked.

Travis and Rob looked at each other and glanced at the cookies and flowers.

"Yeah, we'll be your friends. Nice cookies," With that, our rough friendship began. Travis and Rob took a cookie each before joining Carter and Robyn on the stairs.

I couldn't understand how Audrey and Carter could judge Travis and Rob so quickly, without even getting a chance to be friendly. Friends are friends and a summer with friends is a summer to remember. And that summer was definitely one to remember.

We began this new friendship by sitting on the

Marvinsons' front porch and munching on cookies. We laughed and smiled, everything seemed to be fine until Travis asked the question we didn't want to answer.

"So, can we hang out with you guys all summer?"

"Sure," I said hesitantly. Carter and Audrey shot me a dark look, but there really was no other answer to give them. Travis and Rob smiled and continued to gobble down the cookies. It was unknown to them how much was changing in just a few hours. Audrey frowned and sighed, upset at the whole situation. She wasn't upset about Travis and Rob, they were both actually pretty awesome. She was upset that it was over.

CHAPTER SIX

"Allison! Robyn! Lexie! Wake up! It's Chore Day!" Grandma called to us, waking all of us up with one yell. It worked every time. "Chore Day! Let's go!" Chore Day, the worst and most unpleasant day of our visit. Robyn, Lexie, and I slumped solemnly down the stairs, slowly trying to avoid what was coming.

Chore Day allowed Grandma to feel like she was teaching us good morals and habits while also gaining a clean house in the process.

"How long this time?" Robyn asked sleepily.

"Well, it's not called Chore Day for nothing," Grandma said, wide-awake. We frowned, taking seats at the kitchen table. "What do you want for breakfast? You'll need something hearty to get ready for the work!" We each chose something different to eat; Lexie's being the most elaborate.

"Grandma, I want French toast waffles with

buttermilk cream and three perfectly picked strawberries," Lexie smiled.

"Okay, got it," Grandma said playing along. "Is it alright if the buttermilk cream was just regular cream?"

"That's fine," Lexie said in her baby voice. "Just remember the strawberries."

After we ate, it was time to get to work.

"Okay now, Allison you've got the stairs, hallways, and attic; Robyn, the kitchen and basement; Lexie you can help me with the living room and dining room. Let's go!" Grandma clapped her hands and pushed us along. Just as I was about to climb to the attic, we heard the doorbell ring. Robyn and I raced to get away from work and to see who it was. I got there first.

"Yes, who is it?" I asked as I pulled the door open. Standing in front of us was Audrey, Carter, Joshy, Travis, and Rob. They'd come to play.

"Let's go," Carter said, pulling my arm. "I want to go show the twins the Wolf game."

"We can't," I said miserably.

"Oh? Why not?" Rob asked.

"We can't go because we gotta do chores all day. We'll meet you guys later," Robyn answered for me. Lexie gulped and started to cry.

"Le-kie. Play!" Joshy clapped. His pronunciation of words was so cute. Lexie shook her head sadly and followed Robyn back inside. "Le-kie?"

"Lexie went inside to work, Joshy," I told him. Carter, Travis, Audrey, Rob, and Joshy left with grim looks on their faces, disappointed at the bad timing of Chore Day.

"We're going to have to go to the treehouse without you!" Audrey called.

"Go ahead," I muttered.

"Guys ready to clean?" Grandma asked excitedly.

"No. This is going to be super boring," Robyn moaned.

"Terribly boring," I chimed in.

"Then get started so you have more time to go outside and play," Grandma took Lexie's hand and pulled her to the dining room. I went up to the attic, my first priority, and Robyn started with the basement. Our tradition was if we found anything cool or exciting, we'd share it with each other. That summer, we were both assigned the two coolest rooms in the house.

The attic held secrets of the past, with every old notebook or photograph, a new story blossomed. A story with new questions; questions that we never dared to ask. Questions that we just wondered about; we made up our own elaborate stories to fill in the gaps. I snuck out my notebook and recorded some of the things I found in the attic: an old clown shoe, some baby-doll clothes, a broken mirror, and trunks of Grandpa's old rock collection. My favorite part was trying to find photos of my mom as a little girl, or looking through Grandma's mountain of antique hats. Robyn loved that too, but this year she got the basement.

The basement held precious memories, like the attic, but in a different way. Mostly the recent past ; meaning junk. The good thing about looking through junk is that you might find something that was overlooked or thrown away without any thought. When we were younger,

Robyn and I would sneak down in the basement at night, looking for clues; clues about nothing really. I guess now, it seemed silly to act that way, but when you're young and curious, nothing really stands in your way and your imagination can take hold of any idea.

"Ready?" I asked Robyn as she opened the door to the basement.

"Yeah. You ready?"

"Of course. I want to read some old diaries. Good luck," I smiled. Robyn playfully held her nose, making her cheeks puff up, as she slowly climbed down the stairs. I ran up two flights of stairs, up to the attic. At first, it was dark and scary. After I found the light switch, everything was much clearer. My eyes adjusted to the dim lit room, and I grabbed a broom that was left in the corner. The attic looked exactly like Grandma had left it last year, old and mysterious. Clutter filled the floor, and cobwebs filled the walls and ceiling. It reminded me of an old haunted house that I read about in a mystery book. I guess it didn't get clean it too well last year.

"Get to work, Allison!" Grandma called, seeing that I was just standing there at the top of the stairs. I had set out a plan in my mind. After turning on the air conditioning, I was to attack the boxes and sort through them. Next, I would pick up the clutter from the floor and place everything in the boxes, and if I found anything interesting I would leave it aside to show Robyn later. Once the boxes were done, I would go and attack any cob webs left and finally vacuum. Then I would clean the stairs on my way down and finish the hallways. Be done by lunch.

"Alright," I muttered to myself with a heavy sigh as I opened the first box. "What do we have in here?" The first box was filled with scrapbooks. They were filled with pictures of people, but I didn't have any idea who they were. "Probably all dead," I muttered. The pictures looked pretty old.

Through the tiny attic window I saw Carter, Audrey, Travis, and Rob start climbing up the tree.

"They better save some games for me." I hated working, but I loved it at the same time for different reasons. I hated how this work took up most of my day, but I loved how I had a big adventure up here, alone. I always did my best creative thinking when I was alone. I yanked out a scrapbook and laid it out in front of me, flipping through pages and pages of unknown people. I stopped at one page to examine who was in the picture. For a second, I thought it looked like a young Grandma. I laughed when I saw my mother, her hair was just so puffy; it seemed like it would make a good pillow.

Then there were some pictures of my Grandpa's old cats, like Smoothie. Smoothie was a cat that my Grandpa had when he was still just dating Grandma. Grandpa had loved that cat probably more than he loved gardening or collecting rocks. When Smoothie died he was 20 years old – very old for a cat.

"Allison, are you working?" Grandma asked, just checking in. I hadn't realized I'd been procrastinating, but her voice broke my daydreaming. I instantly closed the scrapbook and pulled out the next couple, arranging them in color order, and placing them in the box neatly. Once they were all in, I pushed the box to the back corner of the attic and grabbed the next box. That box was filled with clothes – old smelly clothes. I pulled out the first piece of clothing, a big flowery hat. Next was a coat, old and full of holes.

"I don't wanna know where that came from," I gulped and stuffed it back in. I didn't want to go through the box anymore, so I pushed it to the door to deal with later.

Soon I had gone through all eight boxes, except for one. I slowly opened the last box, happy with my progress so far.

On the top of the box was a envelop that read Eugene Griffin in black marker. Inside was an obituary. I knew that Ms. Griffin lived alone next door, but I never saw her or knew anything about her. All I knew was that she lived on the left side and Audrey and Carter Fergus lived on the right, that's it. I slowly read the obituary, nervous at what might come out from it.

It read:

Eugene Donald Griffin died on December 25, 1998 being 66 years old. Griffin was born on January 13, 1932. He is survived by his widow, Beth Griffin, and his only child, James Griffin. For most of his life, Eugene worked as the head chef at the local restaurant, Maddie's Own, which ranked 23rd on the best restaurants in town. He went to school in North Carolina, before moving to Buffalo, New York in 1942 when he was ten. He stayed there until his death. Amigone Funeral Home will hold his funeral on January 1st, 1999 at 7 o'clock.

For a second, I couldn't understand what I read. I began to wonder what else I didn't know about Ms. Griffin, and why my grandparents would keep this cut out obituary stuffed up in an attic.

I decided I didn't want to read anything else that might shock me, so I quickly sorted the box and pushed it in line with the other boxes that I sorted. Asking Grandma about it seemed like the best decision.

"Grandma," I paused and second-guessed my decision to bother her with something this silly. Why should I ask her about this? It was none of my business. Besides, I was only three days old when he passed away.

"Yes dear?"

"I, uh, finished the boxes," I told her, finding it difficult to form the words.

"Good, start the cleaning now," She told me, going back to work. I grabbed the envelope that held the obituary of Eugene D. Griffin and pulled the obituary out. I stuffed it into my pocket to show the others later.

"Okay, where's the dust pan?" I called, clutching the broom in my hands.

"In the corner." Grandma hurried back to the dining room, and I went to the corner, opposite of the boxes, and began sweeping away dust, dirt, and cobwebs. As I did so, my mind was still with the Griffins. Minutes flew by, no, possibly hours. It felt like I was up there all day until Grandma called us for lunch.

"Robyn! Allison! Lexie! Come on, sweeties! Hard work deserves a nice lunch!" I raced down the stairs, trying to beat Robyn to the table. Lexie was already seated at the small, round table in her big-girl highchair, smiling smugly. I sat down just as Robyn came up from the basement. She sat down next to me and moved her face close to my ear.

"You find anything?" She whispered to me. I nodded slightly and pointed to my pocket. "Well, I didn't find anything, except junk, like always." She sighed and leaned back in her chair.

"I found an obituary," I whispered back.

"What good is that? It's, like, about death," she made a face and turned around.

"I'll tell you more later. I'll even show you too," I tried to explain as Grandma entered the room, her notepad flopped over in her tired hand.

"So? What do you want? Aunt Stella! Grandpa!"

Aunt Stella hurried and sat down when she heard her name being called.

"Sorry, Mom. I'm just trying to finish up memorizing my lines. The show's tonight."

"It's already lunch, where did this day go?" Grandpa muttered taking his favorite chair at the head of the table

"It went where all the other days go, behind us," Grandma told him. "Orders?" She asked impatiently.

"I'll have leftovers, I can get it. I've just got to get back to work." Aunt Stella pulled open the fridge and grabbed what she wanted. She ran upstairs, back to her bedroom to practice.

"Grilled cheese, please," Robyn said.

"Me too," I added.

"Me three!" Lexie giggled.

"Not me," Grandpa yawned and grabbed a yogurt from the still open fridge. "Just this," he said and closed the fridge.

"No." Grandma pulled the fridge open again and pulled out leftover steak. "Here, you'll eat this too." She had always acted motherly to him.

"Fine." He placed it in the microwave and set it on high.

"Can we be done now?" I asked.

"No, you haven't even had a thing!" Grandma started the grilled cheeses over the stove.

"Not that, can we have a break from cleaning?" I clarified my question.

"Well–"

"Yes! Thanks Grandma!" I jumped off my seat, and pulled Robyn outside. We took off running, knowing that this might be our only chance to escape.

"What about your lunch?" Grandma called to us, but we were already in the Fergus's backyard.

"I'm gonna beat'cha!" Robyn yelled out of breath. I sped up, but she soon caught up to me with her long skinny legs. We ran all the way to the treehouse, where Carter, Audrey, Travis, and Rob were hanging out.

"Hey Rob! Audrey! Carter! Travis! Down here!" I called to them, waving my arms in the air. They peaked down, and smiled.

"Come on up!"

CHAPTER SEVEN

We climbed up quickly, enjoying every minute of freedom.

"About time you came. I thought you'd be cooped up all day!" Carter fist-bumped me, before Robyn rejected and gave him a half-smirk.

"Yeah, I didn't know what you were doing in there," Travis laughed.

"Cleaning. Lots and lots of cleaning," Robyn told him flatly. She flopped down on the wooden boards and leaned back against the tree.

"I'm so happy you guys could come! We were just about to go to the trampoline!" Audrey shouted happily. "And I was tired of being the only sane one here," she murmured to just Robyn and me. The boys climbed down fast and started sprinting to the trampoline.

"Wait!" I stopped them. "I have to show you guys something. Something important."

"What? What is it?" Rob asked irritated that I interrupted his flow of running.

"It's an obituary," I told them.

"Ew! Why would you show us that? It's like a death notice! Yuck!" Audrey screeched.

"It's not that gross, it's just a piece of paper that tells where and when a person died, and tells people when their funeral is going to be. That's all," Travis explained intellectually.

"Exactly," I chimed.

"Who's it for?" Carter asked, ready for a new mystery.

"Ms. Griffin's husband."

"Ms. Griffin? I thought she was a widow," Audrey said stupidly.

"No duh! She's a widow now, because her husband died," Robyn hit her head and sighed.

"Doesn't she live next door to your grandparents?" Carter asked, still more intrigued than the rest.

"Yes," I said. "I want to find out more about her. She always stays hidden in her house, it's almost creepy. I wonder what she does all day, you know, being all by alone."

"I bet she spends all day watching soap operas," Carter laughed. "That's what my grandma does!"

"Maybe she just knits!"

"Yeah, one giant blanket," Audrey rolled her eyes.

"C'mon guys!" I smiled and moved their excitement into action. "Don't you really want to find out who she is now?"

"Yeah! Let's do it!" Carter agreed. Soon everyone

joined into the idea of finding more about Ms. Griffin and her son.

"We should ask Grandma," Robyn suggested our first steps in gaining background information about the hermit-like Ms. Griffin.

"No, she wouldn't answer. Besides, if we go back there she'll put us back to work. Let's try to stay as far as possible from Grandma," I protested.

"Then what are we going to do? Who are we going to ask?" Travis asked.

"Why not Ms. Griffin herself? Who's better giving information about Ms. Griffin, than Ms. Griffin?" Rob guessed.

"No. Ms. Griffin is old and creepy. I'm afraid of her." Audrey shook her head objectively.

"Oh yeah!" Carter shouted. "I forgot to tell you. We found candy again." I opened the brown bag. Inside was one piece left for me. "There were six pieces this time," he told me.

"I bet its Mrs. Marvinson." Robyn nudged me. "She's probably trying to help her kids make new friends."

"It couldn't be," I shook my head. "Mrs. Marvinson wouldn't have given us four pieces yesterday if she thought Travis and Rob would be with us. She would have given us six."

"Who else could it be?" Robyn laughed. "It'd have to be someone who lives here. Someone who could watch us all the time and know when to put the candy here."

"Grandma?" I suggested.

"Probably," Robyn shrugged. "For now, just enjoy

this candy."

As I savored the cherry candy, my mind wandered back to Mr. Griffin's obituary. As interesting as it may be, I felt bad that old Ms. Griffin had lived alone in that big house for more than ten years.

"Well, I think it's worth a shot," Carter smiled after I brought up visiting Ms. Griffin again. "I doubt she'd be mad if we asked about Mr. Griffin."

"Are you serious? She'd be totally hurt!" Audrey crossed her arms.

"We can't be too obvious. Remember, this is a secret mission. We should act like it is her birthday!" I said, thinking of random ideas to get information out of Ms. Griffin.

"Nah, that'd be weird. Let's act like we're really religious. Then we can act like it is a big religious holiday where you go and ask questions about other people!" Robyn joked.

"Now that's just really weird!" Audrey started climbing down the ladder; she didn't understand sarcasm.

"Audrey! Don't leave!" I called to her, but it was too late. Audrey was already off the ladder by the bottom of the tree.

"I'm not gonna be part of this. It's just too weird. Good luck creeps." Audrey ran inside, leaving us with one less member.

"Well, that was very pleasant." Rob smiled.

"Yeah, glad she's gone. She's really annoying," Travis agreed.

"Try living with her," Carter rolled his eyes.

"So are we going with this religious plan or not?"

Robyn giggled.

"No way! Like Audrey said, it's too weird and way too obvious," Carter said, agreeing with Audrey's strong opinions for once.

"Well? What are we gonna do?" Robyn sniffled.

"Simply show her the obituary and ask about what it was doing in the attic," Rob suggested.

"I guess that could work." I shrugged.

"Let's go then. Allison, you'll have to show her the paper," Rob told me.

"I know you'll be the best at this, you're great at making friends." Travis winked and we began our way over to Ms. Griffin's front door, all a bit nervous.

"Did you guys have anything nice for lunch?" I asked, trying to take our minds off of this feeling of intimidation. We all had different expressions on our faces. Rob looked strong, like he was going into a battle he knew he could win. Travis looked like he was about to take a big test, gulping and sweating with multiple shakes in between. Carter looked like he was going to wet himself, but he always kinda looked like that. Robyn just looked irritated, like someone was poking her and they were about to get it.

"Yeah. We had peanut butter and jelly. Brownies too," Rob told me. He didn't look at me when he spoke; he looked to the distance, marching onward in his Converse sneakers.

"Did you save any for us?" Robyn whined. I could hear Grandpa's lawn mower in the background. I guess I'd forgotten to go outside and work with him yesterday.

"Nah, Audrey ate like three!" Travis laughed. "But

we did try to bring some for you guys."

"Of course Audrey would eat ours," I yawned. We were approaching the small red house that belonged to Ms. Griffin, mysterious old Ms. Griffin. As we climbed the stairs together, my hand trembled with the thought of actually meeting her. I took in a gulp of air right before knocking on the old rusted door.

I knocked three or four times, waiting for answer, but no one came out. I was about to tell everyone that we should just leave when Robyn pushed through our small huddle group, and rang the doorbell.

"Come on Ms. Griffin! Pick up!" Rob yelled as if she was on the other line of a phone.

"She can't just pick up. She's an older lady. Her hearing is probably pretty bad," Travis said.

"Or she's just dead. Let's go," Rob spat, irritated from all this waiting and no answer. "I think we should go back up in the attic and look for more clues in the box. That's gonna be much, much easier than trying to talk to dead Ms. Griffin."

"I can't think of anything better to do. Hey, Allison, do you think that you still know that box, the one that had all of those papers of obituaries?" Travis asked me.

"Well, it wasn't just a box filled with obituaries. It was a box filled with papers on different people. Marvin D. Griffin's obituary was the first paper on top. I grabbed it and ran, pretty much." I explained to him. He smiled; either he didn't understand what I meant and just wanted to be friendly, or he had a plan.

****

"Where have you guys been? Come back to work?" Grandma sighed as Robyn and I marched through the kitchen, back up to the attic.

"Yeah," Robyn lied. "We've brought some volunteers to help finish the attic with Allison." Grandma nodded seeing Travis, Rob, and Carter follow us in through the backdoor.

"Oh! You must be the two new kids in the neighborhood. Do you like it here?" Grandma cooed.

"Yeah, it's pretty good. Lots of friendly people," Rob said. I was unsure of whether or not he was being sarcastic.

"And how are you Carter? Where's your sister?"

"Back home, she didn't want to be part of this mission, or, uh, not mission, just cleaning experience," Carter muttered, trying to cover up his mistake. He blushed and quickly caught up with us.

"Mmm, hmm. Mission or not, you're very nice to help clean up here," Grandma went back to work; she didn't really mind what we were doing. Yet, the look on her face reminded me of a sad puppy. It made me feel bad, like I wasn't doing enough to help. Then again, she never accepted any help. She was the alpha dog of this pack. She controlled it all, from the basement to the attic.

"What exactly are we looking for?" Carter asked, when we knew that we were all alone.

"The Griffin code, that's what." Robyn laughed. "Let's see if we can find anything else on Ms. and Mr. Griffin and their baby son, Jimmy."

So it began, the afternoon of sneaking and scanning

through unusual information about random people. We first began with the eighth box where I found the obituary. Each of them had a turn to search to their hearts' content through the box and every box, having detours here and there to try on funny hats, or massive jewelry. We laughed together and worked together, knowing that this was just another crazy day adventure, and when the day was over, we probably wouldn't care anymore.

"Anything?" I called for the seventh time, while I browsed through a 1986 issue of Time magazine reading the old news and searching for clues. Nothing.

"No," They said in unison. I giggled at what Carter tried on; a big flowery hat with pictures of birds pasted to the side. I thought it would have been my grandmother's hat, because of her interest in gardening and birds – all kinds of birds.

"I think I found something!" Robyn called out suddenly.

"Really? Let me see it!" They raced over to where I sat, in the corner on top of box number three. I read a little farther in the passage Robyn pointed to, but soon I saw that the word Griffin was misleading, just saying that there was a new brand of Griffin soap. Great.

"Never mind," I sighed and flopped the old magazine down, grabbing another one from the bottom of the box.

"We aren't getting anywhere," Travis moaned.

"Yeah, tell me about it! I've been through box number seven like a thousand times. I hate this so much!" Robyn moaned.

"Then," I said trying to keep the hope level as high as it could be. "We should try different boxes, ones we haven't been through yet."

"This is getting lame. I'm out," Carter whined.

"Please Carter!" I started, but I glanced out the little attic window just as he was about to hop down the stairs. "Wait! Look! Ms. Griffin is pulling into her driveway! I can see her!" The attic was like the library, producing no real information, just snippets here and there that we had no time to paste together. Ms. Griffin would be like the internet, providing information without the hassle.

Through the window, I could see Ms. Griffin getting out of her car, plastic white shopping bags in both hands. She placed them down on the ground and grabbed some more from the trunk of her car.

"I think she just got back from getting groceries!"

"Then let's go! Better than sitting in this dump." Carter sprang to his feet and hurried down the stairs. Travis and Rob followed him the same way, so Robyn and I were left in the attic.

"By the way, you'll have to clean this up later." Robyn raised her eyebrows and followed the others down the stairs.

"Look at this mess!" I gasped looking around the attic. The attic's cleanliness completely shifted from the way I left it earlier. The organization system was totally broken. Books, magazines, and newspaper clippings covered the floor, no place to step. Old dresses and hats hung from the rafters. Someone had been playing dress up. Carter.

I stood up off my box and climbed my way down the

overflowing stairs. I secretly shut the attic door and locked it up with my hair clip. Grandma wouldn't be able to get back in until I have time to clean up what I'd started. I couldn't hear the silent footsteps of Grandpa as he snuck around the corner.

"What were you doing in there?" His voice startled me.

"Oh, um, nothing," I stammered.

"Ah," he nodded sarcastically, pointing slowly to the door. "What're hiding behind there, Allison?"

"Nothing," I said again, frightened that I might never escape his pointed cross-examination; the questions were bound to melt me some time. I flipped and tried to hurry down the stairs, before he could ask me anymore questions but he blocked my way. He leaned against the side wall with his arms folded, tapping his index finger on his elbow as he judged me with his eyes.

"I said, what are you hiding behind there?" His stern face took away all my will to run. He eyed me with his bright green eyes, enveloping me with his question, like I could never escape.

"And I said nothing, except for all the boxes that I sorted and cleaned out," I boasted. I stood strong, not giving in to his questions. I wouldn't let them break me. I had another mission to focus on.

"Ah," he grumbled, not truly believing my explanation. "Your friends just scurried out of here. Better go catch up with them." He let me go without further questions. I hurried to escape, still feeling his eyes on me, always suspicious. I pushed through the back door and saw the figures of my friends hurry over to Ms.

Griffin's front yard. Robyn was nowhere in sight. I ran to meet them, and soon passed them. They were still running when I got to Ms. Griffin's door.

"You can run really fast, Allison," Travis told me when he met up with me.

"Thanks," I smiled. "Where's Robyn? She left before me, didn't she?"

"Yeah, she decided to go and hang out with Audrey. We're losing motivation," Carter complained.

"I can tell. You guys were practically falling asleep!"

"Well, we aren't really getting anywhere," Carter shrugged. "I'd rather watch TV with Joshy than talk to an old lady about her dead husband."

"It's a mystery, Carter! Let's just go talk to her." *Knock, Knock*

"Hello?" Ms. Griffin opened the door shyly. She was short, gray curly hair, with sweet blue eyes, and red rosy cheeks. "Oh, Allison Brice, Carter Fergus, and who may you two dashing boys be?" She smiled. Though she was practically a stranger to me, she greeted us like we were family that she'd missed forever.

"My name is Rob Marvinson and this is my twin brother, Travis," Travis and Rob shook hands with old Ms. Griffin.

"What may I help you with today?" She asked us sweetly. At that moment, I couldn't find the words to ask the questions politely, so I pushed Carter in front of me.

"Um," he started, embarrassed already. "Well, uh, we were wondering if we could help you garden." Carter mumbled, definitely alarmed to be put on the spot so suddenly. He gave me a glare, but I didn't focus on him. His little side track on the gardening would lead us to more work, but it gave us a chance to talk to Ms. Griffin and really get to know her. For that, Carter was a genius.

"Oh, how sweet! Well, that would be very helpful. As I keep growing older, it gets harder for me every day to bend over with a shovel and hoe. My grass just never stops growing. What a nice group of children." She led us out into the backyard, hurrying us through her somewhat small, cramped house. She smiled as she walked us to the shed, handing us an old, used shovel, stinky fertilizer, and budding flowers. "I've missed having children around. Come, I'll show you the garden."

CHAPTER EIGHT

"Ms. Griffin? What do you mean by missing having children?" Travis asked. He was ready to squeeze the information out of her and finish up this mystery once and for all.

"Oh my," she sighed, "I once had a little lad of my own, sweet Jimmy. That's what I mean."

"Where is he? Can we play with him?" Carter asked stupidly.

"Oh, heavens no!" She giggled at Carter's silly question. "He left home a while ago. Besides, he's a grown man now. You wouldn't want to play with him. Grown-ups are usually boring to play with." She yawned and pulled out a yard chair. She sat watching us work.

"You should really get in contact with him. Children hate not having a mommy or daddy," Rob told her from experience.

"Well, he only has a mommy," Ms. Griffin huffed.

"No daddy, well, not anymore." Pulling information out of her was easier than I'd expected.

"What do you mean? No daddy?" Carter asked.

"Oh, you children are bringing such bad memories to an old sick heart," Ms. Griffin sighed, but continued on with a story. "My husband died on Christmas in 1998, that's why I don't celebrate many holidays anymore. How come you guys are so curious?" She looked up.

"We're just trying to make conversation," I told her, saving us from telling her what we found in our attic.

"Oh that's nice; it warms my heart to see such hard-working children. I'll tell you a story about Jimmy if you'd like." She rolled up her sleeves and leaned back in the chair, letting the sun warm her pale skin.

"Sure!" Carter said.

"Good, then." Ms. Griffin began. "When Jimmy was about your age he came out here and dug up three dozen of my beautiful tulips. He gave them to me on my birthday, silly boy. I was never angrier in my entire life," Ms. Griffin sighed before continuing. "Jimmy was born in 1975 to a happy couple of 10 years. A miracle it was, what a surprise after all that waiting and praying. I was married to my now deceased husband in 1965. I was just twenty years old! Oh, those were the magnificent '60's and '70's!" Ms. Griffin gleamed, reflecting on the memories of the past. I secretly wrote down everything she said in my pocket notebook, making sure each detail matched. I felt kinda creepy, but this was good material for my book. "I guess I could say that my Jimmy Griffin took my husband's gardening tools, on my birthday, and snapped a couple of those beautiful, magnificent flowers.

He handed them to me later that night, with a gleaming smile on his face. What an innocent smile it was. His dad wasn't going to stand for it, oh no! I was mad too, but I was delighted at how splendidly easy it was to look that boy in the eye and say to him the sweetest words in the world. I love you." Ms. Griffin paused for a seemingly long amount of time. "Well, the love business is over now. It's been over since he left for college. I'm sorry if I speak too much, it's nice to have company." She sighed and rocked back and forth in her lawn chair.

"You should get back in touch with him!" Carter exclaimed happily.

"Oh, heavens no! My, I wouldn't want to bother that boy. Mind you, it is a pleasant thought, though, Carter," She said, seeing the disappointed look on his face. "It's just that I can't reconcile with my own son. Silly, I know, but even so, it makes sense."

"Thirty-seven," Travis blurted out, looking up from his flowers that he was digging in.

"Excuse me?" Ms. Griffin looked confused.

"Jimmy Griffin would be thirty-seven right now because he was born in 1975." Travis explained. "It's basic math, just subtract the year he was born from the current year."

"My! Thirty-seven! The last time he visited me he was barley twenty-five!" Ms. Griffin looked grim. "More than ten years of his life I couldn't experience with him. Dear me, why am I spitting my life sorrows in the ears of these children? God help me." She leaned back.

"Ms. Griffin, it's okay. It's good to talk about things that make you sad." Rob comforted her.

"Here," Ms. Griffin said, taking her mind off the subject, "I'll go bake some cookies. Exactly what time will you children need to be home by?"

"Er, six. That's when dinner is put on the table." I told her. Carter, Rob, and Travis nod with me, agreeing with the time.

"Oh, good. We'll have time to make the cookies, and eat them!" Ms. Griffin hurried back in the kitchen. "Do you children want to help?" She poked her head out thorough the door.

"Sure," Travis said standing up, shaking off the dirt from his jeans. We joined him and followed Ms. Griffin to her blue kitchen to start baking cookies.

"Which type would you like to munch on?" She asked us, putting on a tight red apron around her chubby waist. She handed each of us one and I wondered why she would just have four random children's aprons in her house.

"Chocolate chip cookies," Carter said, obviously not concerned or curious to why Ms. Griffin had so many child-sized aprons, or children's gardening tools.

Ms. Griffin slipped upstairs, and she returned with an armful of cooking supplies.

"Perfect, I have everything we need. Oh, put these on. They are just so cute!" Ms. Griffin cried, placing little chef hats on each of us.

Children's aprons, tools, and now hats? I tried not to think about how strange it was to have them just lying around the house. I didn't want to upset her any further by asking about it.

I could tell that Travis and Rob were having the

same thoughts because of their confused and surprised looks every time Ms. Griffin pulled out another random thing. Carter didn't seem bothered at all. Maybe there was more of a mystery to Ms. Griffin than we thought. This wasn't just a detective mission anymore. It was a spy's mission.

"Um, Ms. Griffin? Why've you got so much stuff? Are these all Jimmy's?" Rob asked, flopping around in his large child size apron. Ms. Griffin went red and seeing that she was embarrassed, Rob bit his tongue.

"Well, you see, I-I," Ms. Griffin stammered. "I just, it's, well, not exactly..."

"Never mind, Ms. Griffin, I was just wondering." He continued what he was doing, stirring up that batter for the cookies while Travis and I took turns pouring in ingredients. After Ms. Griffin's red cheeks calmed to her pale tone, Rob shot me a worried look.

"Something's weird," Travis whispered to me.

"Isn't this fun?" Ms. Griffin sighed. There was definitely something strange about Ms. Griffin. Something we hadn't known before.

"Yeah, what time is it?" Carter wondered. Ms. Griffin glanced at the clock, smiling with delight.

"Just 5 o'clock. We have plenty of time!"

"Great," Carter muttered.

"You're not excited?" Ms. Griffin looked hurt.

"No, no, no! I'm very excited!" Carter said with thumbs up, still not sure if he was being sarcastic there, but Ms. Griffin seemed to take it as a sincere response. She giddily smiled and wiped her forehead.

"Now, stick that into the oven and bake it for fifteen

minutes. My, it's so delightful to have children in this old house once again. Jimmy use to bring his friends over, doing homework and what not. It put a big smile on this very face." Ms. Griffin pointed to her own face. She seemed to really revel in the past, every little detail of it.

Once the cookies were placed in the oven, we fell to talking again.

"Ms. Griffin, tell us another!" Carter shouted, when Ms. Griffin's story ended.

She leaned back in a red kitchen chair, seeming to recall several memories before she began. "Here's one: It started on a day much like this one, bright and sunny, a very typical summer day. Jimmy and my dearest wanted to go fishing, down by the old Thompson River. Not much of a river, more of a large stream. I'm sure you know where it is. Anyways, they set up a little corner of supplies, digging up worms and hooking them to the line. It was such fun! They were laughing when Jimmy caught his first fish, crying when he lost it, and smiling again when Eugene tried to teach him how to fish like a pro. Well, the problem of this story is that Jimmy got upset because he never could keep a fish on his line. My husband was hauling them in, one by one, easier than ever. Jimmy would start crying again and again, and I'd have to tell Eugene to slow down on the catching. Jimmy solved the problem on his own, by acting like a bear – he just clasped that fish in his hands once it came in!" Ms. Griffin was so into her story; she clasped her hands like bear claws. "Jimmy smiled and told us that we'd have to cook that fish for dinner. I told him that he won the award for 'the most creative fisherman.' So, I made him an

award-winning dinner for an award-winning boy! Ah,
yes, that was a day to remember." We sat in awe,
mesmerized by Ms. Griffin's amazing storytelling.

"Tell us again," Rob begged, almost whispering his
words.

Ding

"Oh, my! I believe that's the cookies. Who would
like to be my taste tester?" Ms. Griffin struggled out of
her seat, breathing heavily once she was out.

"I'll be the taste tester!" I called out, excited to taste
what I'd helped create.

"Oh! I wanna be one!" Carter shouted.

"Now, now, Allison asked before you did, maybe
next time dear. I'll keep that in mind," Ms. Griffin
smiled, her sweet granny smile. "Here you go Allison."
Ms. Griffin gave me a fresh cookie, not too hot, just
perfect; warm and gooey.

"Oh, wow," I mumbled, my mouth stuffed with
cookie. "It's delicious." My mouth was hungry for more.

"Wonderful! Splendid! Here, each of you can take
some home with you. My, it's almost six. Don't spoil
your dinner." Ms. Griffin packed some cookies in four
different baggies, handing one to each of us. "Share
them." She urged us to the door, seeing that the time was
six exactly.

"Thank you, Ms. Griffin! It was loads of fun!" We
called as we climbed down her unstable stairs. Ms.
Griffin closed the door with a big, grateful smile across
her face.

"Well, that was interesting. We planned on staying
just a couple minutes and ended up staying for a couple

hours," Rob said, eyeing the cookies dancing in his plastic baggie.

"I had fun," I told them. "Ms. Griffin is just a lovely old woman. But," I stopped, trailing off, "I couldn't help notice all the odd things she had in her house; almost too much random stuff."

"Yeah, yeah, yeah. We'll worry about the details later. I think we accomplished more than we hoped for today," Carter ignored me, because like Rob, he was hungry for a cookie.

"Allison! Get here this minute!" Grandma called from the yard over. I sighed and quickly said my goodbyes to the others. I ran to the backdoor and faced her bravely.

"Yes, Grandma?" I asked politely.

"Where have you been all day?"

"I was over at Ms. Griffin's," I told her truthfully. I didn't feel like I had to hide that.

"Ms. Griffin's? Don't you know anything?" She pulled me inside and sat me promptly at the table. She leaned over and whispered in my ear, tickling the hair around it. "Ms. Griffin is as crazy as anything. Please be careful. You never know what to expect from her. One minute she's a sweet old lady, talking about her past. Then, quick as a snap, she explodes in tears of sorrows, or worse, anger." She leaned back, letting me absorb all this information she had just spit in my ear. I didn't know if she was trying to scare me, or giving me an order not to go back.

"She seemed alright. I liked her. She baked cookies with us," I smiled holding up the bag of cookies.

"Oh, dear, that's where it all starts." Grandma sighed, taking a sip of tea. "She loves children. But because her own Jimmy left her, she can't seem to move on. Heck, I bet I've had more contact with Jimmy in the past five years then she had in over twenty!"

"How do you know Jimmy?"

"Why, I was the one that told him to leave," Grandma shrugged.

"Why would you do that? That's horrible!" I asked, a bit angry at her for telling Jimmy to leave sweet, old Ms. Griffin.

"I was doing the right thing. I didn't want Jimmy to get caught up in her 'storage ideas'." Grandma gossiped. "He wanted to go to college somewhere far away too. He just wasn't sure if it was the best idea when he saw that his mother's condition was worsening."

"What do you mean?"

"Well, let me just ask you one question. Does Ms. Griffin seem to have a ton of useless things for daily life at her house?"

"Yeah," I remembered all the things, children's things that seemed to appear out of nowhere.

"Ms. Griffin has a secret. Aa very sad secret that I found out from Jimmy a while ago. I must not tell you now. We're running late to see your Aunt Stella's show. Some other time," Grandma glanced at her watch to check what time it was. She rushed to the stairs and called for everyone to get ready. I followed her, curious to know what she meant by Ms. Griffin having a secret. I thought I'd figured out everything I could about Ms. Griffin.

****

I dressed in my blue blouse, and tight skinny jeans; the same skinny jeans that Grandpa called 'too old for a little girl like me.' Aunt Stella left early to get to the final practice for opening night. Robyn wore her red t-shirt and a pair of purple shorts. Lexie was in her green dress, looking like a little antique doll.

"Is everyone ready?" I tugged on Grandma's sleeve as she spoke.

"Grandma," I tugged harder. "Grandma."

"Not now, Allison." Grandma breathed. "Oh! Did we forget the camera? We need that to take pictures after the show! Come, on! Let's get in the car, I'll run to get the camera." She hurried back inside, leaving the car running.

"Grandma, I know where it is!" I yelled to her.

"Good, then. Fetch it for me. Let me just check..." I rushed by her before she finished, grabbed the camera from the upstairs bathroom counter and continued back to find her. She rested on a kitchen chair and was glancing over the check list.

"Here it is Grandma." I set the camera in front of her.

"Thank you dear. I must find the, oh, what's it called?" She snapped her fingers, as if to try and recall something. All I wanted to do was ask her about Ms. Griffin, but she seemed distracted, fumbling around for an object she couldn't even name.

"Grandma? Can I ask you a question now?" She shook her head and hurried out to the car. I sighed and followed her out, like a sad puppy only wanting a treat.

"Hurry Allison! We're going," Grandpa called from the shotgun seat. I climbed in the back, and sat next to Lexie. Lexie sat in the middle, Robyn on the left, and I sat on the right.

"Aren't you guys excited?" Grandma asked our dull faces.

"Yeah! Well, at least I am," Robyn shrugged, eyeing me curiously. With my mind overwhelmed with information, I couldn't form the smile that Grandma had wanted. I twiddled with my fingers and tried to think of what Ms. Griffin's secret was. It stuck in my mind, overpowering everything else, until only I could think of just that. My face started to burn from the pressure of my hurting head and my endless waiting. All I wanted was for Grandma to tell me what I wanted to know and give me this answer that I was craving. A secret. Ms. Griffin's secret – the secret that kept me waiting and in such anguish.

When we got to the stage show, all I wanted was to at least sit through it without thinking about Ms. Griffin, but that was highly unlikely. I knew that my aunt worked so hard for the past couple days to memorize complicated lines, but it was such a struggle for me to take my seat and listen to the actors speak. My mind was somewhere else, but I sat back and tried to focus.

"When all are lost, in those big towns of the West, there is still them country folks, waiting for their chance to get what they want in life." The first actor with a long black beard said in a strong fake country accent.

"My, I tell y'all Joe. I reckon my life is just waiting to start! Y'all wait an' see!" The second actor with a mustache called out, pulling out a gun from his pocket. *"I'll be a shootin' me some o' those train robbers! I'd be the best darn cowboy of those parts!"* He ran off the stage, in a crazy, happy manor.

"Nah. Boy, I wouldn't waste my time with them foolish cowboys. No. I'd be a wise old business man, smart with money." The third man with full face of hair said. He rubbed his fingers together, as if to hold the money in his hand.

"What's up with all these guys and facial hair?" I leaned over to Robyn.

"It's a western, get over it," she snapped.

"Oh, Charles. You, see? The young ones won't be needing all that money, if you gave them just a little loving."

I recognized the actress's voice. Aunt Stella played the part of Agnesse, the overworked wife of Charles Hardy. She worked at home, taking care of her six children – Joe, Hank, Fanny, Martha, Jane, and Peter – all below the age of fifteen. The whole plot of the story was the travel of a big family to a big town in the west from a small country farm.

"Dearest, can't you see it? A world out there, callin' your name. Wishing for you, dear Agnesse, to live in a wonderful big city. Where all the country folk, go and start a new, joyous life. We gotta go," Charles fantasized as he swept Agnesse from her feet, in a big bear-hug. I heard Grandpa grunt at the sight of Aunt Stella in an almost romantic moment.

"Well, I suppose we could try." Aunt Stella's character blushed. *"But I ain't gonna be hearing about them children crying and whining. That'll be yours, along with your money,"* Agnesse snapped.

"Dear me. A whole new life!" Charles shouted with joy.

The curtains closed and reopened. The ending of the scene brought me back to the real world, remember? The secret? I stretched my arms out in front of me, restless already.

"Pa? Why we gotta go?" One of their children whined.

"Oh, Hank. You and the rest of ya'll need to know something," Charles leaned down, as if to whisper, but stopped halfway so he could project his voice. *"We ain't coming back."* The character of Hank began to cry and held on to his mommy, my Aunt Stella.

"Oh Charles, you bad thing!" Agnesse hit Charles in the arm, as if Charles was a spoiled child. *"Come, Hank."* She pulled Hank out of the scene, holding his arm tight.

"She ain't getting it," Charles began his monologue that I could tell would be long, just by the way he sat down on a barrel. *"All my life, I wanted a nice fancy house, much of them cattle, and a nice loving wife that'll do my bidding. I know Agnesse will get along, soon enough,"* Charles shrugged, pulling his jacket around him tighter. *"She just doesn't know. Doesn't know how long I've been waiting for a chance. A chance to see the world. Her and them babies, they don't know anything. And I wanna teach them. They could have the experience of a*

lifetime. The beautiful mountains, the big adventure. The stuff I heard from all those men who've done the traveling. It seems just so amazing. And the money, oh, the money. All of the money." Charles walked off stage, curtain closing and opening again.

"This is a story that you all will hear one day, mark my words. A story that was strung throughout the ages. From my granddad, to my father, to me, now to you my children."

An old man stood on the stage, standing in front of five children.

"Ma and Pa are waiting for us. Make it fast, slug," One rude child spat.

"My, you children these days. It wonders an old man's heart at how children these days got to be such rude beings." I laughed silently at the dialogue and wondered whether this was part of the script or whether the actor threw in his own ideas about children. The character cleared his throat and began again. *"Here's the story, if you all want to listen."*

"We ain't got time, com'on Fanny, Jane, Joe, Martha. Bill's already with Ma and Pa." The oldest brother pushed the young children along, ignoring the sad look from the quiet old man.

"Peter, ain't we gonna listen to that old man?" Fanny, the youngest asked sweetly.

"Nah, that man's a crazy. We ain't gotta listen to him," Peter pulled her along.

"Hey! Come back here! I ain't got them legs like I use to. I'm just an old man with a story to tell," The old man left the stage. Agnesse and Charles appeared,

looking more hectic than ever.

"Where have you children been?" Agnesse called frantically.

"With that strange old man," one child said.

"Well, we must be a gone, by now! Come on!" Charles yelled.

My mind started guessing about the way the play would develop, and I felt a connection to the poor old man. He had a secret, I just knew it by the way he spoke the word story. Like Ms. Griffin, the man spoke his lines in a sense that he was hiding something, something that was right there but couldn't be grasped just yet.

From then on, it was just another play with a few songs in between the scenes. It had the same typical plot as any other; a problem, a climax, and finally a happy ending. My aunt was great as always. I knew by the way she became her character, I even forgot she was my aunt for most of the play.

In the end, the family arrived in the big town of the west with only losing one horse in the long journey to get there. Agnesse began to see Charles's perspective and Charles began to see Agnesse's perspective. The last lines were as cliché as ever.

"Oh, Charles! We made it! We really did!" Agnesse said cheerfully. She kissed Charles and smiled.

"I knew we would! Oh Agnesse, our dreams are finally coming true! Finally coming true!" They smiled and hugged, ending the performance.

My only problem with the play was the old man. He never came back on stage. His plot was never developed. His secret was never told, and I was left wondering what importance he had on other characters, or if he had any importance at all. I was left hoping that Ms. Griffin's story wouldn't end as his did. I wasn't going to be Peter, and drag others away from understanding her situation.

Grandpa was snoring right as the curtain closed, so I had to nudge him awake. "Oh! What? It's over?" He grunted, gaining a few laughs from the some of the audience close by. Grandma sighed and whispered in his ear.

"Darling, our daughter did an amazing performance, too bad you missed it," she laughed when she heard his response, a snore. I nudged him again.

"You'd be tired too if your usual bedtime was 7:30," he chuckled. After taking pictures with Aunt Stella in her costume, Grandpa and Grandma took us out to the car. Grandma drove us home, smiling.

"What a pleasant little performance. I really enjoyed that. Aunt Stella did an amazing job as Agnesse. I felt like she really was angry at Charles in the beginning, what a perfect girl for such a strange part." She started chatting and would have kept up the whole way home with little statements like that if Grandpa hadn't interrupted.

"Dearest?" Grandpa asked sweetly, before she could continue.

"Yes?"

"Be quiet, I'm trying to nap." He leaned back in the seat, avoiding the hurt look from Grandma. His voice was gruff, less sweet than before.

"Sorry," Grandma murmured. She looked troubled in the rearview mirror. "How are you Allison? You look like you've got something on your mind." I realized that my face still held the troubled, curious look from when Grandma first mentioned Ms. Griffin's secret. I looked around the small, worn out van; Lexie and Grandpa were asleep. This was the perfect time to ask about it.

"Grandma?" She looked back up to the rearview mirror, for a brief second, and then her eyes drifted back to the road.

"Yes, dear?" She smiled.

"What did you say about Ms. Griffin? A secret?"

"Oh, right," she sighed, getting comfortable in her seat. "Allison, it's a long story." She obviously didn't feel like talking about it, which made me just want to know more. I scooted up in my seat, urging for her to tell me.

"Grandma, please tell me."

"Okay Allison, I'll tell you," she said. "But, later." I sighed leaning back in my seat. I got the sense that later meant never.

CHAPTER NINE

"Allison? Aren't you sleepy?" Grandma yawned as she climbed the stairs to bed. I shook my head, even though I could barely keep my eyes open. I was determined to stay up until Aunt Stella got home.

Around midnight, Aunt Stella quietly opened the front door and peered into the darkness of the house. She didn't see me.

"Auntie?" I asked so tired that I sounded dead. She jumped at the sound of my hoarse voice, and she cautiously approached me, with a smile on her face.

"You're supposed to be in bed, little sleepy head." She helped me up from my position on the stairs. It made me feel like I was five, waiting for Santa Claus to come down the chimney.

"I've been waiting for you," I mumbled, about to fall asleep right in her arms.

"How come?" Her voice sounded sweet like a dream

I wished to be in.

"I have to ask you some questions."

"If it's about the play, I'm not answering now, maybe in the morning. It would be silly to answer them now. Come on, it's late."

"No! I'm not going to bed until I know! You can't possibly think that I would just go to bed, after waiting so long, without these questions answered!" I demanded. I was more awake than ever, and my head pounded with adrenaline. My sleepiness had vanished and I wouldn't fall asleep. I could only see Aunt Stella's silhouette in the dark living room, but I could hear her hesitate.

"Fine," she sighed and sat down on the stairs. "What do you want to know?"

"Ms. Griffin. I want to know about Ms. Griffin." I focused, my eyes fixed on the faint outline of her face.

"Ah, Ms. Griffin has a very long and confusing history in this life. I couldn't tell you everything in one night – maybe in the morning," She yawned.

"You just have to tell me now." I frowned and by her expression, I knew my stubbornness won her over. She sighed, grabbed my hand and ushered me to the comfort of the living room couch, knowing we'd be there for a while. She leaned back and began her interpretation of Ms. Griffin's life story.

"Well, my earliest memory of meeting Ms. Griffin was when I was around five. It's weird because I still remember looking into her sad eyes. I went with Grandpa to drop off Ms. Griffin at the hospital so she could visit Mr. Griffin. He was sick and he had been sick ever since I was born. I don't remember what with, but very sick all the time. I was just a silly kid. I had thought Ms. Griffin made Mr. Griffin sick and that she could make me sick too," Aunt Stella laughed.

"What was Ms. Griffin like back then?" I asked.

"Ms. Griffin is a little older than Grandma. I think she's 68 now, so it's been a long time since Mr. Griffin passed. I remember her being a nice, quiet lady, and she probably wasn't that old, but when you are a little kid, anyone over 10 seems old. I remember Ms. Griffin never coming outside, never being that social. Well, that's how she was after Mr. Griffin's death," Aunt Stella said and paused for a moment.

"How about Jimmy?" I asked, breaking the silence.

"To me, Jimmy was the big mean boy on the block," Aunt Stella laughed. "He was much older than me. He was more spoiled then anyone I've ever seen before. Eventually he moved out and left Ms. Griffin. I think he went to college, but it still cut her deeply. I think he was either in his late teens or early twenties, but I can't remember exactly. Jimmy was her precious little baby, and she didn't want to let go of him."

"Why does Ms. Griffin have so much kid things in her house?" I asked.

"What? How do you know that? Allison, have you been down in her basement?"

"No, why?"

Aunt Stella's silhouette of a face turned away and glanced around cautiously before continuing.

"After Jimmy left Ms. Griffin was lost and lonely. I think she needed something to fill the void in her life," she sighed, standing up. "That's all I'm gonna tell you tonight, have sweet dreams."

She left me there, even more confused than before. I had no other choice but to sleep and worry about Ms. Griffin tomorrow.

I slowly climbed into bed, trying my hardest to not upset Robyn's sleep. I held my sheets tight to my body, hoping that I'd figure out this secret mystery soon, before I threw my entire summer away just thinking about it.

CHAPTER TEN

"Allison Brice!" Grandma called out my full name crystal clear. I bumped my head as I sat up, hitting it against the top bunk. I pulled off my covers, and slowly ventured towards Grandma's voice. "Come here this instant!" She was standing right in front of the door that lead upstairs into the attic.

"Yes, Grandma?" I asked, already knowing what she was going to say. I rubbed my eyes, brushing my fingers through my tangled hair. I sighed, leaning against the wall.

"Allison," She sighed, placing her hands on her hips. "Yesterday wasn't a day to go looking for clues about stuff that doesn't matter," she huffed. "Now, I want you to go there and finish cleaning. You don't get breakfast until you finish. I expect you to hurry." I nodded sadly and opened the door to the attic. Grandma started down the stairs, but turned around. "Oh, and Allison, your punishment is that you are forbidden to play with Audrey, Carter, Robyn, Travis, or Rob today. Maybe go outside with Grandpa? I'm sure he'd like that." Grandpa was probably the one who snitched on me. Why would I want to go work outside with him? This seemed to be the start to a horrible day.

"Hey Allison," Robyn laughed.

"Robyn," I acknowledged her presence, but I slipped in to the attic before she could mock me. I wanted to start the day over again.

"Ugh, we left this place a mess," I moaned when I saw the sight of the disaster. The room was filled with magazine clippings, newspaper clippings, photos, open boxes, and other random things that we thought would help us uncover Ms. Griffin's secrets. But, this was a silly mess made by children. Children with nothing better to do. I groaned and sat down on the largest box. I was already bored out of my mind.

To put myself in a happier place, I decided to simply think about something I enjoyed. I cleaned up thinking about those treehouse gifts. They too were a mystery, just like Ms. Griffin. If I wasn't allowed to find out more about Ms. Griffin, then I'll just find out more about those little presents.

"Allison, you working?" Grandma called from downstairs.

"Yeah," I sighed, moving wisps of hair from my face while I worked.

"Come down, Allison," she ordered. I placed the newspaper I was folding in a box and headed down to meet her. "Grandpa is going outside right now. I want you to clean yourself up. Get dressed, brush your teeth, comb you hair, that sort of thing. I expect you to be out with him today. I know it will be fun for both of you." Grandma hurried away; a broom in one hand, a basket of laundry in the other.

I tried to make the journey to my room as slow as I could.

"Allison? You coming?" I heard Grandpa call to me. The back door slammed shut a moment later, so I figured that he just went outside instead of waiting for me. I quickly threw on my old yellow t-shirt and a pair of my work jeans. I ran to the bathroom and tied my hair in a knot. I pulled it out to make a nice bump-free ponytail.

"Coming, I'll be right there," I answered Grandpa's call, but I wasn't even sure he was inside. I dragged on my socks and my dark blue sneakers, and ran outside to meet him.

The air was cool, cold for summer. I saw Grandpa over in the garden, working on some blueberry bushes.

"Allison! Over here!" Grandpa waved his arms in the air, shouting to get my attention. I hurried over to see him and start my so called punishment.

When I began working, I started to understand that I overreacted. Even though I wasn't getting to spend the day with my friends, I got to spend some quality time with my Grandpa. Grandpa wasn't so bad. He was actually fun to work with. The only problem I had was the growing grudge against him for telling on me.

"Grandpa? Did you tell on me? About the attic?" I stopped, feeling like the only way to let go was to ask him.

"Oh, Allison," He sighed and I waited for him to continue, but that was his only response. It gave me mixed thoughts, but I decided to just put it out of my mind. I was right to be punished for leaving the attic the way I did, and it didn't matter who told Grandma.

"No, no, don't pick those quite yet. They need more time to grow," Grandpa told me as I started toward a different patch of berries. "And remember, never pick the berries that the birds have gotten to," Grandpa gave me a word of advice. I always admired how much he knew about everything.

"Grandpa? What do you know about Ms. Griffin?" I asked.

"Ah, isn't this the question that got you in trouble in the first place?" Grandpa smirked.

"Yes, but I thought you would know. I just thought it would be something to talk about while we work, that's all."

"Uh-huh. That's all, that's all," he mumbled off, repeating and chuckling about what I just said.

"Well, do you know anything about her?" I persisted.

"Oh, yes. By far, I know a lot."

"Then will you tell me?" I asked again.

"Nope. Nothing."

"Please? Oh, pretty please!" I pleaded, my hands folded in prayer position. He grinned and chuckled with his usual okay-you-got-me smile.

"Well, I'll just tell you this. Jimmy left for a reason. There that's all," he continued his gardening work as if nothing had happened. He began humming to himself and

I felt like I shouldn't try to beg him anymore.

In my head, I kept replaying his last words, trying to decipher them without my head exploding. Jimmy left for a reason. Jimmy left for a reason. Jimmy left for a reason. What reason?

I knew that I wasn't going to get any more information out of Grandpa just yet, so I stayed quiet until my work was done.

"Allison! Time for lunch!" Grandma greeted me as I hurried back inside. "See, I told you that working with Grandpa would be a lot of fun." She noticed my happy smile and red, sunburned cheeks from working. "I made you a PB&J sandwich. I know that Robyn doesn't really like them very much, but I thought you did. So, here you go!" She handed me lunch.

"Thanks," I said placing the plate down on the table and went to wash my hands.

"Allison, I found this memory book that I thought you might be interested in. I don't believe it's any of your business, but as you worked so hard, it's a book filled of pictures of Jimmy and Ms. Griffin after Mr. Griffin died. We were great friends with them."

"Are you still?" I asked admiring the ancient, blue photo book.

"No. Well, not as much as we use to be."

"Is that why Jimmy left?" I asked trying to squeeze more information out of her.

"Oh, Allison! Stop it! I didn't want to answer any of your silly questions, so stop making me," she huffed.

"Where's Aunt Stella?"

"She's over watching Joshy and Lexie at the

Fergus's. Why?"

"Oh, no reason," I answered. I plotted to go there right after lunch, if I could sneak out. "Could my punishments for the day be over? Like now?"

"Over? Now?" My Grandma's expression changed suddenly. "Well," she hesitated.

"Oh! Great! Thanks Grandma!" I sprung from my seat, not letting her finish. I raced out of the house.

"Allison! Come back here!" I could barely hear her and I ran even harder. I ran faster than I would racing against Carter, faster and faster.

"Man, Allison! You look like you just escaped from a bear attack," Aunt Stella exclaimed as I ran through the Fergus's front door. Through the window, I could see Carter, Audrey, Travis, Rob, and Robyn playing on the trampoline.

"Almost," I said with a smile. "Grandma was holding me hostage."

"That explains it!" Aunt Stella laughed. "I have to watch Joshy while their mom is out. What do you need?"

"Information," I said bluntly.

"Oh no, not this again," Aunt Stella sighed, picking up Joshy and holding him in her lap.

"Just one, tiny question? Please, oh pretty, pretty please!" I begged her. "Grandma left me hanging for this question to be answered!"

"Alright, hit me." Aunt Stella gave Joshy a block and he threw it on the ground.

"No. Dat one." Joshy pointed his fat baby fingers at a different toy and Aunt Stella handed it to him.

"Better now?" She asked him sweetly. He nodded,

shaking all his hair onto his round face and sucking on the toy block in his hand.

"Aunt Stella!" I begged her again. "Please listen to me! I'm desperate."

"Then ask me already!" She placed Joshy on the floor and sat with her eyes only focused on me. "Okay. I'm ready."

"Well, then here it goes," I cleared my throat. "Did something happen to Ms. Griffin? What's so wrong with Ms. Griffin that it made Jimmy leave?"

"Actually that was two questions."

"Oh, just please answer them! I'm desperate!" I cried.

"You're so silly Allison. Why do you even want to know?" She took my hands in hers, smiling at my curiosity.

"Please! Once I hear a mystery, I just can't think of anything else until it is solved!"

She sighed, taking her hands away and making her face darker and darker.

"We found out several years ago when she asked us to water her plants while she was away. Grandma and I went over to her house. We didn't want to miss any of her plants, so we checked everywhere, even in her basement... It was just so unreal," Aunt Stella's story continued. "Everywhere piles and boxes of stuff. There were even shopping bags full of things with the tags still on them. Little passageways were the only ways to get around. For most of the time we had to push our way through all the junk. It was horrible. It wasn't like extra storage like Grandma's attic, it was not healthy. Ms.

Griffin didn't know we found out about her little secret, but she started getting the clue after a while. We just didn't know what to say. Grandma made me promise not to tell anyone, except a doctor if the time came. She's a hoarder, Allison. You understand what that means? She keeps stuff she doesn't need, she buys things she doesn't need. She can't let go of stuff. She has a mental illness that is exhibited by her actions of hoarding. That's why Jimmy left for a college far away. I doubt he could stand living there much longer. I shouldn't be telling you all this, don't tell Grandma, okay?" She breathed heavily like she'd finally gotten a load off her chest. I nodded with my mouth wide open. I was shocked and actually kind of horrified. Ms. Griffin, a hoarder? I had seen reality shows on TV about hoarders, but Ms. Griffin didn't seem like she had a problem. Her kitchen and living room were spotless, yet I hadn't seen her whole house. Her garden was kept tidy too, but I didn't know about the shed.

I went home, not sure what to think. This was why Grandma didn't want me to know or have me over at Ms. Griffin's home. I felt a horrible, uneasy feeling, like I wouldn't be able to see Ms. Griffin in the same light ever again.

I needed to get out of this mindset of being so focused on a secret I wish I'd never learned. I wanted to escape this new knowledge and go back to what summer was really about, no worries.

"Allison! Over here!" Carter called to me as I left Aunt Stella. I went through the backdoor and was planning on doing a loop around the house to contemplate what I had just learned, but Carter's shrill voice lifted me from a state of melancholy.

"Come on! We're playing Wolf!" Rob encouraged me. I shrugged and leaped on the trampoline with ease.

"You can sit here," Travis smiled at me.

I was beginning to like Travis and Rob. Both had proven to be a great addition to our summer adventures, and not the losers we first thought them to be.

"Did you find anything in the treehouse today?" I whispered to Travis.

"Yeah, six pieces again," he smiled.

"Really? Who had my piece?"

"Robyn," he laughed.

"Any leads?" I ask him.

"Rob and I think it's Carter and Audrey's mom, but they deny it. So, I guess we don't really know."

"Ready to start?"

****

As dinner grew closer, my thoughts about Ms. Griffin grew rapidly. I didn't talk during dinner or speak up by asking questions either. I just wanted to focus on one thing, tomorrow. I think Grandma could sense what had happened, so she didn't pressure me to clean up after dinner or go to bed. She let me do what I wanted, and that was very nice.

"Hey Allison! Tell Grandma what happen at the trampoline! It was so awesome!" Robyn pestered me, but I just stared off in space because I couldn't help thinking about Ms. Griffin. "Come on Allison! Tell Grandma the joke that Audrey made about the twins and how Rob just lost it! It was hilarious! Everything's okay now, though, of course."

Robyn ignored my silence. I just sighed, knowing that I was the one that kept them all from killing each other. I didn't have the energy to put up with anymore small talk.

"I'm going to bed," I announced. I kissed Grandpa and Grandma, hugged Aunt Stella, Robyn, and Lexie goodnight. Robyn frowned and traced the outline of her plate with her fork.

"Are you mad at me?" she mouthed.

"Why don't you finish your steak?" Grandma asked to keep me down.

"Don't like steak very much," I shrugged.

Before heading upstairs, I glanced at Aunt Stella. She was looking down at her plate, not eating much herself. I never wanted her to feel guilty, because in all honesty, I should be blamed for the way I was feeling. My continuous begging caused her to finally tell.

CHAPTER ELEVEN

I stayed in bed until ten thirty. I didn't want to wake up and confront what was waiting for me. It felt good to just relax my head, emptying it from all the Ms. Griffin drama that I'd gotten myself into.

My scratchy yellow blankets were tangled at my feet, and the more I struggled the tighter they squished my toes. The air in my room was muggy and hot, and I kept debating whether I should get up to have a drink of water or not.

After a good ten minutes of arguing in my head, Robyn came in to make the decision for me. Grandma was finishing the last batch of pancakes.

"Hey Allison! Wake up!" Robyn marched into our shared room with her pink Hello Kitty slippers. I acted as if I wasn't awake and kept my eyes closed, but she caught me when I cracked a smile. "C'mon Allison," she grumbled under her breath.

I shook my head, so she shook me until I fell out of bed, crunching my nose on the floor. "Gosh, you're so not a morning person," she muttered and slammed the door on her way out. The carpet was softer than I expected, so I just stayed there for a few minutes, imagining what would happen if I stayed there forever.

My crunched nose started throbbing, so I picked myself up from the ground and checked my nose for blood. The sound of my heart beat pounding from my nose vibrated through my ears, but I could still hear Robyn complaining to Grandma that she just couldn't wake me up.

"Allison?" Grandma called, coming up the carpeted stairs in her white apron. "Do you want any pancakes?"

"No, I'm fine Grandma," I called back. "I'll just get dressed and go out with the others. I think I'll skip breakfast today." Surprisingly, Grandma didn't jump at the opportunity to preach about the importance of breakfast to me. She just said okay.

I jumped out of bed, and threw on my clothes. I didn't feel like brushing my hair, but I did it anyway. I forced myself outside and found my way to the treehouse just as the others finished up on the trampoline.

"Anything today?" I heard Carter ask as they climbed up. When he heard my footsteps, he flipped around and jumped off the ladder. "Hey Allison! It's you! You woke up!" He ran over to me and gave me a hug. "I thought you were sick."

"No, you said you thought she was dead," Audrey laughed. Carter pouted, pushing his lower lip to his top.

"Guys! Look! Here is something!" Rob pointed to

the corner of the treehouse where the trunk met the unsteady wooden platform. Six unique yo-yos were stacked in a pyramid. Each of us took one. Travis and Rob took the pair of blue ones that formed the base of the pyramid. Audrey took the pink one on the top and Robyn took the yellow one. Carter took the green one, so I took the purple one. It was the first time the treehouse gifts weren't candy.

"Different." Audrey examined her yo-yo. "But I like different." She nudged Rob with her elbow. I glanced at Carter and he started to chuckle.

"Weird, right?" Robyn whispered to me. "One day she hates him, the next day she's got a crush on him."

"Do you like to yo-yo?" Audrey asked Rob.

"I used to yo-yo all the time," Rob boasted. "I can show you guys I few tricks if you want. I'm really good." He grinned and wound up the thin string that kept the yo-yo bouncing.

"Show us!" Carter yelled and swung his yo-yo around in a circle.

"Well first," Rob stuck his hand out and caught Carter's yo-yo string with one hand. "You should be careful. I don't feel like getting any bruises."

"Sorry," Carter murmured and tangled the loose string into a ball on his hand.

"Mine doesn't work," Robyn whined after multiple tries.

"Here let me show you," Rob smiled.

Rob was really beginning to fit in with the others, but I couldn't say the same for Travis. He was less forward than Rob, but he was a great listener.

"Are you a pro at yo-yos too?" I turned to him as I tried to engage him in the conversation.

"Yeah, but I'm not as good as Rob," he smiled and fiddled with the string. "You slept in late today."

"Yeah, I know," I sighed.

"You seem upset," Travis leaned against the tree branches. "Is something on your mind?"

"Well – " I started.

"Allison! You've got to try this!" Carter hurried over to me and yanked my arm to turn me around.

"Wait, Carter," I told him, "I'm talking to Travis."

"What? You can't tell me?" Carter frowned.

"No, it's not that," I tried to explain.

"Then tell me," Carter insisted. "Tell everyone!"

"Fine, but I need you to promise you'll keep quiet about it," I sighed. I wrapped the purple yo-yo's string around a twig and let it dangle. "It's not something I'd really love to tell everyone."

"You have lice!" Audrey shrieked.

"No, no!" I said as I began itching my head just at the thought of those bugs. I cleared my throat and began again. "Ms. Griffin, the lady that lives next door...," I paused, having trouble making the words form in my mouth, "she's a hoarder."

I pushed the loose hairs away from my face to see their reactions. Audrey wasn't impressed.

"Um, what's a hoarder?" Audrey asked, more focused on the pink yo-yo and the tricks Rob had just taught her. "Is it something bad?"

"No duh!" Carter exclaimed. "It's gotta be something bad, right Allison?"

"Well, it's definitely a problem," I nodded. "It's like a really bad habit."

"A hoarder is someone who takes stuff in and never throws any of it away," Travis said impressively. "Our old foster family had a garage full of old computers, but I didn't think it was a problem until I heard they had gone to meetings with a counselor about their addiction."

"Did they get better?" I asked.

"We left before we found out," Rob said.

"I doubt they'd ever clean out their garage." Travis shook his head. "It was hard to live with them."

"They were going to adopt us too, but when our social worker did a home check, they saw what was in the garage and had us taken out," Rob frowned. "It was a pretty bad experience."

"Well, now you're with us," Audrey smiled.

"Right," Rob grinned.

"So what exactly is a hoarder?"

"It's a mental illness, kinda like obsessive-compulsive disorder," Travis said. "At least, that's what they told us when we were put into a different family."

"The things hoarders collect are seen as really valuable to them, but might not seem like much to anyone else," I continued. "Hoarders lose the ability to throw things away and feel attached to the items they collect."

"That's why it's so hard to convince a hoarder to get help." Travis bit his lip. "At least in our case, it felt like they cared more about their collection of computers than wanting to adopt us."

"Huh," Audrey looked upset. "That's pretty sad."

"Yeah," I sighed and thought about Ms. Griffin.

"I wish we could have helped, but our social worker said it was a deeper problem and something we couldn't fix," Rob said. "I guess sometimes it's just too late to help."

But sometimes it wasn't too late. That afternoon, I was going to Ms. Griffin's house. I'd made up my mind.

CHAPTER TWELVE

Ding, Dong

I barely knew Ms. Griffin, but I knew I needed to accept her. After learning such a dark secret, I couldn't let her live that way. She wasn't an evil person. In fact she was quite kind when I met her before, and for some reason I just felt like I had to help.

It seemed like everyone else in her life deserted her; her family, her neighbors, and any friends that she used to have. I didn't have any history with her, so I thought I could be the one that could be honest.

"Hello? Oh, it's you, Allison! Where are your friends?" She let me into her house.

"They're still eating lunch, I finished early." I smiled as she led me into the kitchen. I wondered if she knew how fast my heart was beating or noticed my constant glances around her house looking for signs of hoarding.

"Would you like to have some cookies? I just took

them out of the oven." I didn't know how to approach Ms. Griffin. I felt like I should ease in to it slowly, with a fact or something, but I wasn't that type of person.

"Ms. Griffin? Are you a hoarder?" I froze, not believing my quick, rude actions. By my blunt question, an embarrassed, depressed look formed on Ms. Griffin's face. Her cheeks started to glow with redness, and the wrinkles that framed the corners of her lips started to quiver.

"Er, where did you hear that? Silly old rumors… is your nosy grandma talking about me?" She didn't look at me in the eye, and turned her back to me after she finished her question. I felt ashamed, but I knew that this was the right thing to do.

"Rumors? Are they just rumors?" I murmured.

"Look, Allison. Do you see my house? Does it look like I have a problem? Take a look and tell me what you see." I turned my head and I glanced over every little detail.

"Well, I guess I see nothing that looks like hoarding."

"See? Just rumors. My, you are a curious girl now aren't you? I love seeing curiosity in girls your age. When my Jimmy was your age…" she started to change the subject, but I interrupted.

"What about the basement?" Ms. Griffin turned away quickly and bit her lip in response.

"Oh Allison, maybe you should just go," Ms. Griffin said with a fake smile. "It might be best if you come back another time."

"But I –"

"Shush, now dear," Ms. Griffin's temper started to rise.

"Ms. Griffin –"

"No, no dear," Ms. Griffin ran her hand through her short graying hair. I knew if I left now nothing would change.

"Please let me help you," I said quietly.

She stared at me with empty eyes.

"How could you help me? You can't help me." she cringed and started to tear up.

"But I want to help you," I urged. "I know I can."

"How can a little girl like you help an old, shattered woman like me? Allison, I've lost so much. I don't want to lose anything more. I can't let go of the things I love." She turned back to me. I could see the hurt in her eyes, the real passion behind her sadness. "I'm not sure why I'm telling you all this, Allison. Please excuse me, dear."

"I understand," I said rushing to her side and helping her slowly into a chair. "I think that the only way to stop this problem is to regain what you lost." I hinted.

"What do you mean? Eugene is dead. I can't get him back. My Gene," she sighed and wiped her eyes. "I can't let go of his things and everything that reminds me of him." She started crying again and stood from the chair to grab a tissue. "It's all I have left of my family."

"Jimmy," I said in a whisper, "Jimmy can still be part of your family."

"You don't understand!" She hollered at me, livid that I brought up such a delicate subject. "I can't tell you how much I hurt!"

I'd never lost anyone I loved, so I didn't have as

much empathy for Ms. Griffin as I should have had.

I glanced out the window and saw my friends out in my backyard. Why couldn't I just be normal? Why did I always have to get involved?

"I'm sorry Ms. Griffin. You're right, I don't understand. I'll just leave, I'm sorry. This is none of my business." I started for the door, my hands stuffed in my pocket. I barely made it two steps before I was tugged to a halt.

"Wait." She bit her lip. "I'm only curious. What was your plan to get Jimmy back?"

"It's very simple, Ms. Griffin. Just give him a call." I sat down, glad that she called me back.

"Oh, no! Jimmy doesn't want to hear me. After his father died, well, it started." Ms. Griffin shook her head and began to breathe heavily. "It started with just Marvin's old things, but slowly it turned into things that I'd bought years ago and never used. I keep thinking that there's some use to them. There has got to be some use, eventually there has to be a use, Allison. I can't let any of it go. What if there is a use for something the moment I throw it away? Oh, I have this burning that tells me I need it. Just the thought of throwing any of it away gives me a headache."

"I bet he wants to hear his mother's voice again." I took her hand to calm her down. "I bet he is just scared, like you are."

She was quiet for a long time, and kept rocking back and forth with her eyes closed.

"Please try it," I continued. "You won't regret it. If you've already lost Jimmy, all you can do now is get him back."

"Well, Allison…" she spoke softly.

"I'll be in the room too, if that makes you feel any better. If Jimmy gets angry, just give the phone to me." She nodded nervously.

"What's Jimmy's phone number?" I asked, unsure if she even knew.

"566-987-2238," she recited by heart. "I looked him up in the phone book." I smiled to myself, knowing that she must have thought about calling him a million times. I nodded punching in the numbers before she could stop me.

"Hello, Griffin residence. Jenny speaking," a child's voice rang in my ear.

"Um, Ms. Griffin? Did Jimmy have kids?" I turned my head, surprised to hear a little girl speaking.

"No, I don't think so. He had a girlfriend in college, but never any children," Ms. Griffin told me and rocked anxiously in her chair.

"Hello?" I said speaking into the phone. "Is Mr. Griffin home?"

"DADDY!" Jenny yelled. "SOMEONE'S ON THE PHONE FOR YOU!" In the background I could hear heavy footsteps coming down stairs.

"Ms. Griffin! Here's the phone," I gasped.

"No!" she shrieked. "I'm not ready! I can't do this!" She began to rock faster, but I pushed the phone against her hand.

"You can do this. You have to do this." She couldn't take the phone. Her hands were shaky and her face was super pale. She jumped up, but I grabbed her hand. "Fine,

I'll put him on speaker phone."

"Hello? This is Jim Griffin." I saw the fear and excitement in Ms. Griffin's eyes. I was nervous for her just the same. I said a silent prayer that this would go well.

Ms. Griffin took a deep breath and looked to me. She stood up tall and confident.

"You can do this," I mouthed. She nodded and closed her eyes.

"Hello? Jim Griffin here," He repeated.

"Jimmy?" Ms. Griffin began to tear up at the sound of his voice.

She began to wobble again, so I grabbed the chair for her to sit. She stared at the phone, waiting for a response.

"Jimmy, this is Mommy," she breathed heavily and slowly. Her shaky hand squeezed mine and her rocking began to slow.

"Mom?" Jimmy's voice was almost lifeless. "Is that really you? I thought you would never speak to me again." Ms. Griffin began to cry in the moment of acceptation.

"Yes, it's me." She could barely make out the words to finish her sentence, and every breath she took was like listening to the sound of an air vent. I could hear cries and mumbles coming from Jimmy too. I felt awkward and out of place, this was Ms. Griffin's moment now.

"I'll leave you guys to talk," I whispered as I started to leave. Ms. Griffin caught me by the arm. She looked at me with eyes of relief.

"Thank you, Allison," she mouthed. The first step of

Ms. Griffin's transformation was underway.

I walked home feeling like I'd accomplished something important. For once, my crazy obsessions paid off and actually made me feel satisfied. I knew all she needed to do was try, and a little push in the right direction had done her good.

Tall, prickly grass tickled my ankles as I walked through her untrimmed yard. I saw my friends playing a few yards away, but I decided to just head back to Grandma's house and catch up with them later.

That evening, I was already half asleep when Grandma finally called us for dinner. My mind was busy with thoughts again and the more I thought about Ms. Griffin, the more I knew I needed to find a way to clean her basement.

The problem was her compulsion to hoard and the feeling of overcoming sorrow she got when just thinking about throwing anything out. I didn't want to push her too far and make her back out so soon. She didn't see her basement as messy, or cluttered with too much stuff like Grandma's attic. She saw her possessions as terribly important to her life. There wouldn't be any way I could convince her. I had to do it behind her back.

CHAPTER THIRTEEN

I started out the day with a bright smile on my face that faded quickly. I had planned to clean out Ms. Griffin's basement, but tons of questions flooded my mind. What did it look like? How long would cleaning take? How would Ms. Griffin act? Was this like Chore Day? Would I have to actually nitpick my way through? I only prayed that Ms. Griffin didn't invite Jimmy over yet. I wouldn't let their relationship be ruined again because of Ms. Griffin's stubbornness. I'd expect Jimmy to get angry if he realized Ms. Griffin was still hoarding.

Everyone else had already eaten, so I hurried through breakfast; gobbling each and every spoonful of my oatmeal.

"Allison? Is something wrong?" Grandma asked me when we were all alone in the kitchen. I didn't want to tell her what I was up to. I was nervous that she wouldn't approve of my plan to dedicate so much time to helping

Ms. Griffin.

"No, I'm perfect," I said putting on a polished smile. Grandma smiled back.

"Okay, if there's something you want to talk about let me know," Grandma said. "You don't seem too interested in Ms. Griffin anymore. I'm all ears if you want to talk."

"I'd rather not," I sighed. I stood from my chair, leaving after inhaling my oatmeal like a vacuum. I slid on my jacket, and headed over to Audrey and Carter's house.

"Oh, if it isn't the brave, courageous Allison," Robyn smirked.

"I'm cleaning out Ms. Griffin's basement today," I stated openly. "Jimmy wants to reconnect with her, but I'd doubt he would after seeing her basement again. I mean, that's why he left! And I bet her basement got a whole lot worse after he left, since she uses it to replace the feeling of love. I have to do it behind Ms. Griffin's back, but before Jimmy comes over for their first visit. You know, so he won't leave again," I sighed. "Would any of you guys like to help?" I knew after I asked their only answer would be no. Each and everyone one them shook their heads in replying.

"Who'd want to clean out an old lady's basement? Yuck!" Audrey frowned.

"You guys should be ashamed of yourselves. If any of you had this problem, you'd want help, right?"

"Well yeah, but we don't have that problem. It's not our thing to worry about." Rob shrugged.

"Stop being selfish, Rob. You can't give up on people just because there is something wrong with them."

They were pathetic for not even trying. I stormed away, livid at the way they didn't care. I was done messing around; even if that meant I'd have to do it alone. I wasn't going to let their coldness sway me.

Ding Dong

"Oh, it's just you Allison," she let me in and helped me slip off my blistering hot coat.

"Why, are you expecting someone else?" I asked, praying that she hadn't invited Jimmy over yet. I was sweating from my armpits down, regretting the jacket outfit immediately. In my mind, I went over different ways I could get Ms. Griffin out of the house. I couldn't have her here while I destroyed the one thing she still had authority over, her hoarding.

"Why, yes I am!" she exclaimed. "Why are you here, dear?"

I didn't want to tell her, but after a moment of silence, I realized that telling my reason would be the only way I could even get in her basement. "I think you should start letting go of things you don't need. I have come on a mission to clean out your basement." Her face formed into a frown the moment I started speaking.

"No, no, no. I can't think about that right now. This is supposed to be a happy moment." She started ushering me towards the door.

"Do you really think that this will be a happy moment when Jimmy asks to see your basement?" I jabbed.

"Shush now." Ms. Griffin's eyes clouded. "You don't understand, Allison."

"Wait! I still need my coat." She eased up and let me

grab my coat. As my hand clasped the hood, I darted past her arm and ran down the hall towards the basement door. I found the stairs when I left her house the other day, hidden behind a coat rack.

"Allison! You get back here!" I ignored her pleas and pulled open the basement door.

Her stairs were impassable, filled with boxes, bags, and piles of stuff. There would be no possible way to fit anything else. If she kept this up, her whole house would be swallowed with things.

"Oh, Ms. Griffin! You need me to help you! You can't go on living like this!" I begged her. I was overwhelmed, and cried at the sight of such a broken disaster. I didn't like what I saw, and I had never been so worried for another person in my entire life. I was crying for Ms. Griffin, and for her son Jimmy, who had to live with this since his father died. "Please let me help you! You don't even have to watch. Go to the store and stay there for a couple hours! Anything!"

"Allison, Allison, please don't cry. I know my burdens and I know who I am. It's my problem to deal with. You don't need to worry about it."

"Yes I do! You won't take care of it yourself! You need help! I need to take care of it! I can't see you living like this! I'd feel responsible for it if you can't get around in your own house. That will be my problem and my fault for not at least trying to help." I wept.

"I understand how you feel. I just—"
Ding, Dong

The ringing of the bell interrupted Ms. Griffin's thoughts. She smiled. She quickly closed the basement door, repositioned the coat rack, and ran to the door, hobbling all the way. I wiped my eyes and tried to look presentable. We both knew who was at the door.

"Jimmy! My Jimmy! You look so different! Oh, how you've grown," she smiled and gave the stranger a hug. He stepped in the house; he was a head taller than Ms. Griffin, and much taller than me.

"And you must be Allison, the one that brought me back to my mother. Thank you." He stuck out his hand, I grabbed it. His shake was firm and strong. "I'm James Griffin, but you can just call me Jimmy." I smiled.

The three of us started talking, but soon Jimmy and Ms. Griffin were just simply catching up on their lives. I wanted to sneak down and clean out the basement before the topic of Ms. Griffin's hoarding came to Jimmy's mind. Jimmy told Ms. Griffin that he was married to a woman named Ida Manson, now Ida Griffin. He has two children, Jenny, and Xavier. He told Ms. Griffin that he wanted her to meet them and be their grandma. Ms. Griffin tried her hardest not to think about our previous conversation, but every now and then I could see the lines of anxiety on her face. She would have to face her problem sooner or later.

I came up with a plan that I put into action when Ms. Griffin excused herself to check on her cookies in the oven.

"Hey Jimmy? Could I ask you some questions?"

"Yeah," he leaned back in his chair.

"You know about your mom's problem, correct?" I asked trying to sound professional.

"I did. She told me that she had gotten over that little

problem in our phone call the other day. Why?"

"It's not little," I told him easily. "Her hoarding hasn't stopped."

"What? I don't see any of her hoarding, no trash, no random objects. I see no problem here," He corrected me as his fingers tapped the thick leather chair. He glanced around the room and nodded. "She's gotten better. You barely know her." I knew what I needed to show him, but inside I was worried I might be doing more harm than good.

"Come with me," I sighed.

Though I felt bad about possibly ruining the mother-son relationship for a second time, I knew that Jimmy would understand. Even though I had hardly known him for thirty minutes, he seemed more compassionate than I'd originally thought.

I led him over to the stairs to the basement. His brown boots took slow, heavy steps against the hardwood floor. I opened the door just a few inches and his expression told me everything.

"Holy... I can't believe this is still going on. It's been so long!" Jimmy backed away slowly, shaking his hands and rubbing the small stubble on his chin. He sat back down in his chair, but his eyes were empty. After a moment, he leaned forward. "I didn't know."

"Jimmy, I have a plan to clean out her basement. Will you listen and help your mother?" I felt mature, talking to an adult this way. I whispered him my plan before Ms. Griffin came back.

"That will definitely work," He cleared the sadness from his face. He was just as determined to help his mom as I was and I liked that about Jimmy. He understood that his mother was not well and that the only way for her to get better was through the love of her family.

Ms. Griffin stumbled back into the room and plopped herself down on her big, ugly orange couch. It didn't compliment the floral wall paper as much as she thought.

"I'm glad to see that you guys are getting along. Well, the cookies are out of the oven, and it's about lunch time, I bet your grandmother would like to see you home about now. Say your goodbyes Jimmy," she instructed, acting as if he was a three-year-old.

"Goodbye Allison," he said loudly. To just me he whispered, "We'll put that plan of yours in action after lunch; I can see now that if I truly want my mother back, I need to be the adult and not run away this time." He smiled to me. "Come around the back and I'll let you in. We can't have my mom getting suspicious." From that point on, I felt like Jimmy and I were the only ones that truly wanted to help Ms. Griffin.

"Goodbye Ms. Griffin, have a fun day with Jimmy," I called as I went out the front door. I ran home, delighted in the fact that someone else was just as fixated on helping others as I was. Ms. Griffin needed us now, and I couldn't let her down. I gobbled up my grilled cheese quickly, not speaking to anyone.

"Hey Allison! You didn't play with us all morning." Robyn grumbled as she came in sweating. "We had races. I won three. I even beat the twins." I nodded, super focused on what I was about to do.

"Then where were you, if you weren't outside

playing with them?" Grandma asked curiously. "You weren't at home, so where could you have been?"

"I was exploring," I said. It wasn't a total lie, I was exploring Ms. Griffin's basement. I couldn't keep a straight face when I lied, so I just kept eating. Soon I had finished my milk and grilled cheese.

"Doubt it," Robyn breathed.

"Anyway," I continued, ignoring Robyn's comment. "I was wondering if I could go out and garden a little bit, later." I had to have an excuse for leaving the house. No one would trust me being alone when they didn't know where I was.

****

I went out of Grandma's house through the dusty, yellowed garage. Grandma had given me the children's gardening gloves that she'd bought earlier in the week. Being the rebel I was, I slipped a box of heavy-duty, black trash bags under my arm. I cared more about succeeding in Ms. Griffin's basement mission than being caught by Grandma.

I slipped behind the deep side of the garden, and waved to Grandma from the window. I wanted her to get a good picture of me working before I tried my great escape. After everything I'd pulled this week, I was under a lot of supervision. After about five minutes, I disappeared. I low-crawled under the fence that separated Ms. Griffin's and Grandma's property, and with the help of Ms. Griffin's tall, untrimmed grass, I made it to the back door without getting caught by either of them. I crouched under the door's tiny window and listened for voices.

"Hey, Mom?" Jimmy asked.

"Yes?"

"I was thinking," Jimmy remembered the plan. "Could we go back to that toy store you always took me to when I was a little kid?" Ms. Griffin's face blossomed. "I know it is all the way downtown, but maybe we can pick out something for my kids?" Jimmy was proving to be more clever than I expected. She clapped her hands together excitedly, ready to embark on one of her great adventures to the store, to buy more… stuff.

"Oh yes! I would love to take you there! Maybe we could get another doll for my collection!"

"Great!" Jimmy smiled, matching her enthusiasm. "but I really want to find toys for my kids, if that's alright." He was a born actor and he knew how to persuade his mom.

"Oh yes, well, that sounds good too." I heard Ms. Griffin. I could tell she wasn't too fond of that plan, but she would go along with it just because of her want to be with Jimmy. They left shortly after with a swing of the jacket; soon I heard the car back out of the driveway. Now it was left up to me. Jimmy's part was to take her out of the house. My part was to clean as much as I could without her noticing. I wanted her to realize that the time she had with Jimmy and her family was more important than the stuff she has kept over the years. I couldn't let her just throw away a lifetime of family for a lifetime of useless junk filling up her small home.

I took a deep breath and opened the basement door.

All I could see were piles, boxes, bags, of stuff. A trash bag in one hand, a pair of gloves in another, I found a spot to start. I slipped on my gloves, and started to fill the trash bag. I was determined. The things I found were junk. A pair of shoes with a hole in them, piles of junk mail, magazines and newspapers, old gardening tools in an old canvas bag, even empty prescription bottles with long expired dates. It was a horrible sight. I couldn't even get down the stairs, and at this point, I wasn't sure that I wanted to. I thought I could get at least one-fourth of the basement done this afternoon, but now I wasn't sure I'd even get past the first step.

"Yuck!" I shrieked when I saw there were mountains of cobwebs in the corner of her step. I ran out to her garden shed and grabbed her bug repellent. By the half empty can, I could tell she used a lot of this stuff.

I hurried my way back inside, spraying the bug poison all over the corner. I was scared there might be some spiders, and I really hated spiders. The only problem was that the more I sprayed the more cob webs there seemed to be. I couldn't do this on my own. Defeated, I took my filled trash bag out to Ms. Griffin's garage and put it in her empty trash bin.

When Jimmy and Ms. Griffin came back after a three-hour shopping spree, I had made it through three steps and filled her entire trash can and recycle bin. I was fatigued and dejected. As they came in the house, I plopped myself on Ms. Griffin's orange couch, leaving all evidence of cleaning behind the closed basement door.

"Allison? What are you doing here? I thought you would have left to go back home." Ms. Griffin was more than curious.

"Oh, I did, but I thought I forgot my coat. When I saw your car pulling up, I decided to wait for you." My lies had been getting better and better.

"Oh, well, you are welcome to stay until your dinner time." Ms. Griffin went to the kitchen, probably to bake some more.

"How did you do? Did you get it done?" Jimmy asked in a whisper.

"Not even a little," I answered truthfully. "It was worse than I thought it could possibly be. I only got three steps done. Also, she has tons of cobwebs. I can't get it done all by myself. You need to help – or I'll call exterminators and cleaners to come and help."

"Whoa," He shook his head in disbelief. "That's a lot. I've never really thought about all it'd take to help my mom. Let's just sleep on it, okay? We'll make a new plan. I'll be back tomorrow, but I'll stop by your house first."

CHAPTER FOURTEEN

I didn't waste any time laying in bed that morning.
My focus was on coming up with a new plan. Jimmy
would be over to discuss with me, and I had to be in the
perfect mindset to figure out what to do. I felt guilty
about not finishing Ms. Griffin's basement the day
before. My mind was overwhelmed from all the
unexpected stress I'd developed since the day I found Mr.
Griffin's obituary.

"What's up with you this morning?" Grandma
served me breakfast in the plastic Strawberry Shortcake
divided plate she'd been using since I was two. Eggs were
flopped over Strawberry Shortcake's rosy, red face. My
strawberries and bananas were in the divisions forming
her floppy hat.

"Nothing too much," I said as I scooped some eggs
up and revealed Strawberry Shortcake's cheeky smile.

"You can tell me anything, Allison." Grandma sat

down, showing her softer side.

"Anything?"

"Anything," She assured me.

"Jimmy's coming over soon," I told her honestly.

"Jimmy? Jimmy Griffin?" Grandma huffed. "What did you do Allison?"

"Nothing!" I cried, but I gave into my Grandma's stern look. "Alright, I guess I did one thing. I fixed Ms. Griffin's relationship with Jimmy."

"What? Why?" Grandma slammed another plate of eggs on the table. "Allison, it's none of your business! I thought we were done with this!"

"We're not, Grandma! Not until Ms. Griffin's basement is cleared out and she gets help!" I screamed.

"You've always been like this, Allison," Grandma shook her head. "You just care too much about problems you shouldn't be involved in."

I was done with all the abhorrence targeted at Ms. Griffin. She was a human being, just like the rest of us, and she had to be treated like one. No one had to suffer like she did.

Ding Dong

"Jimmy!" I squealed. I wasn't even dressed yet. I ran up the stairs and let Grandpa answered the door. I threw on a pair of jean shorts and a polka-dot tank top.

"Well Jimmy, it's nice to see you. Are you in the neighborhood visiting your mom? That'd be surprising, but anyway, what can we do you for?" Grandpa rambled on. He gave me the perfect amount of time to finish getting ready.

"Actually, I came to see Allison," I heard his voice

from the top of the stairs.

"Allison? What for? Did she do something bad?" Grandpa's voice harshened.

"No, no," Jimmy laughed. "I need to speak with her about something important."

"She's a kid. Anything you tell her, you can tell me," Grandpa was about to ruin my chance to redeem myself.

There were a lot of things I had trouble with in the Ms. Griffin situation. I've always felt guilty that I had to go behind Ms. Griffin's back. I never felt so sneaky and tricky in my entire life.

I had to go behind Grandma and Grandpa's back too. They trusted me not to get involved, but I did it anyway. I knew Grandma smelled something fishy after I told her Jimmy was coming over, but I had a pit in my throat for not coming clean about the whole situation.

I felt bad about not spending as much time with Carter, Robyn, and Audrey as I had in the past. They were having their own adventures, probably not as deep as mine, but I was still upset I couldn't share the memories.

"Come on in, Jimmy," I sighed. I thought it'd be the best time to relieve some of my built up guilt.

"Allison, what's going on honey?" Grandma asked me.

"Nothing's wrong," I shrugged. "I just need to tell you guys something." Grandpa eyed me suspiciously, looking from me to Jimmy every other second.

"Allison," Grandpa's voice was stern. Jimmy was silent, but he knew what I had to do.

"Let's go talk in the living room so we don't clog up

the doorway." Grandma didn't seem angry; I didn't feel any vibes of anger like I did from Grandpa. And I knew that Grandpa wasn't really angry as much as he was just concerned.

"You haven't been the same, Allison." Grandpa was the only one who remained standing once we got to the living room. "What's going on?"

Jimmy looked at me, but I couldn't find the right words to continue.

"Allison is helping me get my mom better," Jimmy said bluntly.

"In what way?" Grandpa asked him. "How could she help? I can't think that there is much for a young girl to do around a lady with a mental problem!"

"There are more ways than you'd think," Jimmy tried to explain, but his words were suffocated by Grandpa.

"You explain, Allison," Grandma went gentle.

"I want to help Ms. Griffin clean out her basement," I said.

"She already did a lot," Jimmy tried to pick up where he left off. "She brought me back into my mom's life after many years of silence. I knew my mom had this condition, but I never guessed it'd be this bad. I know I have to help my mom get better, before all of her stuff overpowers her."

Grandpa was silent for a long time. He just nodded his head and paced the wooden floor a few minutes. His long shoes and skinny legs creaked the floors while he thought.

"I think it'd be best if your Grandpa and I had a

private chat of our own." Grandma stood, grabbing Grandpa's arm.

"Just a minute," Grandpa whispered. "I understand, Allison. Helping others is just your nature, isn't it?" He laughed and clicked his tongue before taking a seat on his favorite red leather chair. "You've got a heart on you, dear. A little stubborn and persistent, but you're a dedicated friend." He smiled and leaned back in his chair. "You know what? I'm a bit hungry."

"Have an olive, Grandpa. Those always fill you up," Grandma said.

They marched off together, hand in hand. They had the feeling of family that Ms. Griffin deserved. They left us to talk alone.

"This job is too big for one girl to do," Jimmy said, getting straight to the point. He rubbed his hands together and sighed. "I just don't see how we're going to get this done."

"We need a new plan, that's all. Don't give up so soon," I frowned. I hated it when people weren't as determined as me.

"Well, what do you suggest?"

"We'll confront Ms. Griffin head on."

"I don't know about that," he stuttered, "I'm pretty sure Mom won't like bringing her problem up. Especially not with me, you know, with all our history."

"But you have to!" I begged him. "She's not going to take it seriously unless you're the one who tells her she needs to stop. I know I just met her, but I know she cares about you. She wants family, she wants love! She wants you to be in her life! I know she'd do anything to keep you."

"Alright, I'll do it," Jimmy sighed. "This isn't going to be easy."

"Things like this are never easy. At least, in the long run everything will be for the best." I smiled.

"You're right, I know," Jimmy muttered. "I want my mother to be better, I really do. It's just hard to do this on our own."

"I understand," I told him. "I can find volunteers."

"It's not just that, Allison," His voice cracked, like he was about to cry. "What will happen after we get it all cleaned up? Will she keep hoarding? I can't go through this twice."

"Nah," I tried to calm him down. "You'll need to find her a doctor that can help her through her problems. We just need to do our part and clean."

Jimmy nodded solemnly, his eyes searched the floor.

"Not only that," His voice hardened to a whisper. "We've got to remind her that things don't matter as much as people.

"Right." I grinned. I couldn't imagine the pain that Jimmy was going through. He lived with the clutter before. It was the same clutter that clogged his heart for so long that he didn't want to be in Ms. Griffin's life anymore. I wasn't going to give up.

"Let's go," Jimmy sighed as he stood from the couch.

"Right now?" I gasped.

"Why not? The sooner the better." Jimmy cracked his knuckles. "I'm not going to take her to the doctor without her permission."

"So what are we going to do?"

"Confront her straight on, I guess," Jimmy shook his head. "This is going to be so hard."

I followed Jimmy out the front door and crossed the itchy grass yard to Ms. Griffin's house. He knocked on the door confidently and quickly clenched his fists. He took a deep breath as the door opened.

"Jimmy!" Ms. Griffin hugged her son tightly. "Oh, and Allison. What can I help you with, dear?"

"Mom, we have to talk to you," Jimmy answered for me. "It's about your problem."

"Allison!" Ms. Griffin cried and backed away. "How could you tell him?"

"Mom, please just listen!" Jimmy begged her. She was quiet, surprised at Jimmy's sudden forceful tone. "We want you to get better. I want to help you, Mom. I can't stand to see you living this way and not be bothered by it. I care about you."

"I can't do anything about it, you know that Jimmy," Ms. Griffin cringed. "I'd do anything I could to stop myself for you. I just can't. "

"But you can, Mom," Jimmy protested. "You just have to try."

"What are you trying to get at Jimmy?"

"A doctor, Mom. I want to take you to a doctor."

"We think it'll be the best for you to get over your habit professionally," I added, "and to start fresh with a clean basement."

"Clean my basement?" Ms. Griffin shook her head. "That'll be impossible."

"But you're willing to let us try?" Jimmy pushed.

"Of course," Ms. Griffin conceded and breathed heavily. "If it's what you want."

I sighed, the stress of going behind her back still lingered in my head, but now I knew that I didn't have to worry about her getting mad.

"Mom, I want to be part of your life. I want you to meet your grandkids," Jimmy said. "I just can't have my kids around your house until that basement is cleaned. I don't want them to think of you like that."

"Do it then, but I just don't want to watch."

"You won't have to." Jimmy smiled.

A bell from inside her house dinged, ringing my ears for a few seconds.

"That must be my cookies! You're welcome to some Allison, if you want to stay." Ms. Griffin hurried into her back kitchen.

"No thanks," I called to her, thinking I'd eaten at least three dozen cookies she'd baked in the last couple of days. "I should probably get back to my house."

"I'll take her to the doctor tomorrow, that's when I have off work," Jimmy spoke to me quickly. "I want you to be ready to clean out her basement in two days."

"You want me to have all the volunteers ready in two days?" I was shocked.

"I think it'd be best to start as soon as possible," Jimmy shrugged. "She can start fresh after counseling."

"I'll do the best I can."

CHAPTER FIFTEEN

"Where have you been?" Carter shouted as I jumped the uneven, wooden fence to the Fergus's backyard.

"I've been busy." I shrugged and picked a splinter out of my left hand. I had been feeling guilty about abandoning my friends for Ms. Griffin, so today was the perfect day to catch up on our usual summer activities.

"Get your swimsuit on!" Audrey yelled wildly. "It's time to battle!"

"Ugh, really?" I complained.

"Yep! Back over the fence you go," Carter grinned.

"Let's go!" Robyn turned me around.

"Don't forget to invite Travis and Rob, Audrey!" Carter yelled as he ran into his blue house to get his swimsuit on.

"Why are they coming?" Audrey stuck up her nose.

"I thought you were starting to like the twins!" I rolled my eyes. It was typical Audrey to switch up her attitudes towards people so randomly "They're coming either way."

"Oh come on, Audrey!" Carter hollered from his window. "Just because Rob said you looked funny in your baby photos doesn't mean he doesn't like you!"

"Whatever," Audrey yawned. "They're not joining my team."

"Did I miss something?" I leaned over to Robyn.

"Nah, just Audrey being Audrey," Robyn whispered to me. "I'll race you back to the house."

I let Robyn win, but only because I wanted to catch a glimpse of Ms. Griffin's house one more time before diving right back into an average summer.

Carter ended up inviting the twins himself, after begging Audrey to give them a chance. None of us still had a problem with letting the twins into our group except for Audrey.

Robyn and I slipped in our swimsuits as fast as we could and met the others at the edge of the chilly pool. The heated concrete burned my feet, but we had to stay out of the water until Audrey formally explained the rules to the twins.

Audrey was always prompt and straightforward when giving the instructions.

"No cursing, no biting, no peeing, and no feet," she eyed Carter, "that's a new one."

"Gosh, it's not a big deal," Carter shrugged, but nudged me in the side. "It is totally a big deal."

"Alright, so we're ready to start?" Robyn snapped her swimsuit straps against her tanned skin. "What do the teams look like?"

"Well since it's my house." Audrey twirled her water gun in the air and smiled deviously. "I'm making a new rule."

"It's my house too," Carter frowned. "What's the new rule?"

"There will be three teams instead of two."

"Fine with me," Travis said. "Who's my partner?"

"Rob, of course," Audrey stared at Carter and clicked her tongue.

"Are you mocking me?" Carter pursed his lips. "I know you only made that rule because you don't want to be on their team."

"You didn't want to be on my team?" Rob looked hurt. "Is it because of that baby picture thing? I was only joking!"

"Whatever," Audrey shrugged. "I'm just ready to crush you."

"Positions people!" Robyn shouted and cannonballed into the water. Part of her wave splashed up against the side of the pool and lapped against my toes.

I followed Carter in down the side and took our starting position at the stairs. Having won the last battle, we went in confident.

Travis and Rob were new at the game, but it didn't stop them from taking chances. Once the game began, the new duo team were taking boats, claiming corners, and loading water guns faster than the rest of us could keep up.

"How are you guys so good?" Audrey gasped, out of breath, in the middle of the battle.

"We have to be good," Rob shot Audrey in the face with a blast of cold water.

"Hey!" She wiped her eyes. "Why do you guys have to be so good?"

"We've got some tough competition. We've got to give it all we got," Travis said and refilled his water gun.

"You're tough competition! Who could possibly be your competition?" Audrey asked.

"You!" They laughed and high-fived before swimming off.

"Sure," Audrey smirked and swam back to Robyn.

"Did that on purpose?" I nudged Travis.

"Did what?" He asked, oblivious.

"You know, suck up to Audrey."

"We didn't suck up," Rob claimed. "I think we're getting on her good side though."

"Ha, I doubt that." Travis refilled his water gun. "You can't be sure with Audrey."

"Okay pause!" Robyn called out from the diving board. "New teams! I think it should only be two teams, since Travis and Rob are kicking our butts."

"Fine by me," Carter sighed, flopping underwater for a break.

"Here are the teams," Robyn declared. "Me, Allison, and Carter will be one team and Travis, Rob, and Audrey will be on the other." She flashed me a wink.

"Seriously?" Audrey grunted. "I thought we were teammates Robyn!"

"Ready?" Robyn counted down and ignored Audrey's complaints.

"Hold on!" Audrey pouted.

"Go!" Robyn bellowed without letting Audrey finish and jumped into the pool water. Audrey had to suck it up and begin the battle. She knew she had to be ready to battle at all times, and a sudden switch of the teams would be something she had to deal with to be the best, even if her teammates were her declared rivals.

"Fine!" Audrey screamed and dove under the water before I could shoot her with water.

"This way, Audrey," Travis laughed. "We'll explain our plan to you."

Robyn swam over to where Carter and I had been hiding out. Her head popped out of the water and startled the already tense Carter.

"You didn't see her coming?" I laughed.

"No," Carter replied sheepishly.

"You did that on purpose didn't you?" I smiled at Robyn and glanced over to Audrey's new team.

"Of course!" Robyn boasted.

"How come?" Carter frowned. "This is the first time you ever wanted to switch partners. I thought you and Audrey would be together forever."

"We will!" Robyn laughed. "But I did this for her own good. I just feel like it's time that this group was really bonded. Nothing's going to be fun unless the twins and Audrey start getting along for good."

"So true," I said.

"So what's the plan?" Carter cracked his knuckles.

"That was the plan," Robyn grinned, "and I think it's worked. Look!"

Audrey and the twins were laughing. Not at each other, but together. This was a monumental moment in the history of all summers.

"Wow," Carter gasped. "I guess you're right."

"When have I ever not been right?" Robyn smirked and brushed her wet hair away from her neck.

"Let's go spray them," I whispered.

"What? Why?"

"Yeah, Allison! Why'd you want to ruin a perfect moment like this?"

"We wouldn't be ruining it!" I laughed. "Forcing them to work together to defeat us will keep them bonded. Isn't that how enemies get along in movies?"

"I don't understand, Allison." Robyn crossed her arms angrily.

"Hmm, think of it like this. They're working together to defeat a common enemy. It's like reversing the anger they have towards each other to us," I sighed. "Just trust me."

"I'm in," Carter agreed smoothly. "You're always right, Allison, but Audrey is going to be so mad!"

"That's true," Robyn shrugged. "But I guess we'd have to attack sometime anyways."

"Right," I took in a deep breath before counting down. Robyn and Carter rapidly refilled their water guns and took position to fire. "Be ready to attack in 3…2…1."

****

After the water battle, our two teams joined together to enjoy fruit flavored ice popsicles up in the treehouse. Carter hunched over the railing, dangling his feet off the side. Audrey chose a spot near her slowly accepted friends, Travis and Rob. Robyn and I sat leaning against the big oak tree that sat right in the middle of the treehouse, holding our beloved fortress together.

I really wanted to tell the others about my plans with Jimmy, and my mind kept wandering to more worries about Ms. Griffin. I could imagine Jimmy sitting with Ms. Griffin in a pale white doctor's waiting room, holding her nervous, clammy hands; talking to her for comfort. I could imagine the words of love and support exchanged.

I wanted to be there too, but I knew her mental health wasn't my worry in the plan of everything. Plus, I wasn't going to bring her up in conversation with the others. It wasn't time yet.

"We should get on the trampoline soon," yawned Rob. "I feel like jumping."

"Let's do it," smiled Audrey. "You can choose the game if you want."

"You mean that?" Rob was surprised.

"Sure," Audrey shrugged. "It's no big deal."

"No big deal!" Carter huffed. "No big deal, sure."

"Get over yourself, Carter," Audrey laughed.

"Hey! What's that?" Rob pointed to the corner of the tree.

"Is it what I think it is?" Travis jumped off the ledge and planted his worn sneakers at the edge of the treehouse.

"Be careful, Travis," I muttered. "Falling off wouldn't be very fun."

"Don't worry, I'm fine," Travis said, leaning over the ground structure.

The treehouse's wood boards started to creak as his body slowly slinked lower and lower.

"Travis, I'm serious!" I yelled frantically.

"Almost got it," Travis moaned. His arm reached for the little brown package, dangling from the side of the treehouse. "Got it!" He flopped, right-side-up and scooted away from the edge.

"What's inside this time?" Carter joined him. He reached for the bag with his sticky popsicle stained hands, but Travis yanked the bag away before he got too close.

"Let's see," Travis opened the bag and stuck his slightly dirty hand inside. "Hm, just candy again."

"Just candy?" Carter laughed and reached for the bag again. "That's the best!"

"Have at it," Travis stood leaving the brown paper bag open. He wiped his hands on his shirt and took his seat next to Rob.

"Do you think we'll ever find out who's been giving us this candy?" Robyn wondered. I gulped and looked away. I had a pretty good idea.

"Yuck!" Carter's face turned green.

"What is it, Carter?"

"I think it's been here for a few days," Carter spat. "It's all melted!" He dropped the bag in disgust.

"I bet it has," Travis pointed out. "I had to pull it out of a tough notch it was stuck in. I'm pretty sure whoever drops these presents off didn't mean to put it there."

"Pretty bizarre stuff," Rob sighed and took a seat next to Carter. He put his head back on the fractured wooden bars that supported our treehouse.

"Hey," Travis ran his fingers along the branch we signed our names on each year. "When can we sign?"

The four of us paused for a long time and none of us wanted to answer. The sacred branch would be just one more thing that would be broken with the newcomers. But it didn't seem like a bad thing. The signing of Travis and Rob's names would lift the veil that we'd created to conceal our summer friendship.

"That branch is full," Carter mumbled.

"Hey, you know," Audrey whispered. "We could start a new one."

CHAPTER SIXTEEN

"I'm ready," Ms. Griffin sighed slightly, rocking back and forth in her old wooden chair. "Do what you want with my stuff, I don't need it anymore." She finally gave in after hours of endless counseling with Jimmy's friend, Dr. Hill. Ms. Griffin was an old woman who had finally let go of an unhealthy, tenacious habit.

"Well, I'm glad to hear that," Jimmy sighed; his body was hunched over and he was tired of the fight he'd finally won. His hands were folded together, his fingers clenching and unclenching at a constant pace as he calmed down.

"I don't need things." Ms. Griffin closed her eyes, whispering her new mantra. "I just need love."

"That's right, Mom." Jimmy nodded. He'd grown tired of the topic just as Ms. Griffin had.

"I just need family," She said.

"That's right," Jimmy repeated with a whisper.

His fingertips were against his mouth and his lips moved slowly like he was reciting a silent prayer.

"It's just – " Ms. Griffin's cheeks flushed red and her eyes welled up. "It's just so hard."

"I know, but we can get through this if we stay together." Jimmy took his mother's hands in his and kissed her cheek. "I will do anything to help you."

"I know you would, Jimmy." A tear slipped from her eye as she spoke. "I realize now that I will always have you."

"Don't make me cry," Jimmy sniffed. "We're going to start cleaning up the basement as soon as possible. I've already planned for you to stay at my house while we clean. You can meet your grandchildren, won't that be wonderful?"

"Can I keep just one thing?" Ms. Griffin begged.

"You know that's not healthy," Jimmy objected quickly. He sighed, giving in slowly. "What would you need?"

"A watch, that's all," Ms. Griffin wiped her tears and began to compose herself. "Your father gave it to me on our fifth wedding anniversary. It has our wedding date engraved on the back."

"I'm not sure – " Jimmy started.

"We'll find it," I promised. I wasn't ready to let Jimmy take over completely, and seeing the suffering we'd put Ms. Griffin through in the past days, it was nice to finally agree to one of her many requests.

"Thank you, Allison," Ms. Griffin smiled softly.

"Where would it be, Mom?" Jimmy asked, ignoring the fact that I'd interrupted him.

"Actually, probably not in the basement at all," Ms. Griffin shook her head.

"What do you mean?" Jimmy asked.

"I mean there's more stuff in this house than you think," Ms. Griffin squeaked.

"Oh God, seriously?" Jimmy puffed. "Why didn't you tell us before?"

"Don't get frustrated with me!" Ms. Griffin cried. "I didn't want to tell you because I knew you'd be upset."

"Can you blame me?" Jimmy whined. "That just means we have more work than before!"

"Stop it Jimmy!" Ms. Griffin cried. "I know I was wrong, but you just have to work with me. This is hard for me."

"It's hard for everyone, Mom," Jimmy mumbled.

"It's not like the basement," Ms. Griffin continued slowly. "It's different."

"How so?" I asked. I'd tried to stay out of the conversation as much as possible, in fear that I might be butting in to something that might turn personal.

"I'll show you, how about that?" Ms. Griffin said.

"Er, are you sure that's necessary?" Jimmy asked. "I've seen enough clutter for a lifetime."

"You can show me," I offered.

"Come, Allison," Ms. Griffin stood from her cushioned chair to take me up the stairs.

"Get volunteers while she's at my house over the weekend," Jimmy pulled me aside before I followed. "We'll have to do everything in those two days, do you understand?" I nodded quickly and ran to meet Ms. Griffin at the stairs.

"Where is it stashed?" I asked her once we were out of hearing distance from Jimmy.

"Upstairs, in Jimmy's old bedroom," Ms. Griffin whispered to me.

"So this started after Jimmy left?" I gasped.

"This started because Jimmy left," Ms. Griffin said shamefully. "But it's not as bad as the basement, I think."

At the top of the stairs, Ms. Griffin led me down a hallway until we reached two black-painted doors. Ms. Griffin reached in her pocket and pulled out a rusted brown key.

"I always keep it with me," She said. Carefully, she stuck it into the first door's key hole and opened the wobbly door slowly.

Thousands of plastic bags crowded the floor and furniture. It looked as white as snow, but transparent, and I could see all items inside.

"This breaks my heart," Ms. Griffin's voice cracked. "I'm more ashamed of this than the basement." I picked up the first bag, closest to my feet and reached my hand inside.

"What is all this?" I asked amazed at the quantity of items in each bag. "They all look new."

"These are things I bought, but never opened. Purchased, but never used," Ms. Griffin sang sadly. "I always thought that there'd be a good use for some of this stuff I saw on sale. I just couldn't resist. Some of it reminded me of Jimmy, and other things reminded me of Eugene. A lot of the things, though, were things I thought I'd use someday with my family. The problem was that my family didn't want me. And I bought it all on clearance so I can't return it, even if I wanted to. I just kept bringing it in."

"You know," I started, glancing to each untouched shopping bag. "You can sell this stuff."

"Sell it?"

"Yeah, like in a garage sale," I encouraged her. "If it's never been used, people would pay good money for things like this." I peeked into the next bag; a new spatula, three spiral notebooks, and a toy tea pot.

"You really think so?" Ms. Griffin glowed. "It's like my own business."

"Yes, but a business we wouldn't want to continue," I sighed. "This is a lot of stuff."

"There's more," Ms. Griffin said. She pulled me away from the room of plastic bags and into the room next door.

"More shopping bags?" I gasped.

"I'm a bit of a shopaholic," Ms. Griffin confessed. "Like my counselor said, 'I use things to fill my emotional needs.'"

"What's in them?"

"Oh, just the same type of stuff that's in the other plastic bags," Ms. Griffin shrugged. "Junk now, I guess."

I nodded, creating a plan in my head.. "It might be nice to get a profit from your cleaning, Ms. Griffin."

"Yes, that would be nice." Ms. Griffin smiled. "I'm just not sure who'd be willing to go through all this stuff."

"Oh," I grinned, "I've got a few people in mind."

CHAPTER SEVENTEEN

The plan was set. Jimmy would pick her up on Friday morning and bring her back Sunday night. Jimmy decided it would be best for a dumpster to haul away the junk. He bought cleaning supplies, large trash bags, and gloves for the cleaners. My part would be to arrange the garage sale and take care of finding volunteers.

"Hey, Aunt Stella? I have a little bit of a proposition for you," I smiled sweetly in my attempt to gain a first volunteer that night.

Aunt Stella was over at the Fergus's house babysitting little Joshy. He was up on her knees and she bounced him to the rhythm of his lullabies.

"What kind of proposition?" she giggled, raising one eyebrow playfully. Joshy was chewing on his red fire truck toy, and Aunt Stella had to constantly make sure he didn't try to swallow it.

"It's a big one," I said, trying to be serious.

"Okay, tell me," she focused.

"I need to ask you to help me clean out Ms. Griffin's basement."

"Wait, what?" Aunt Stella's eyes widened and she put Joshy on the ground.

I told her everything.

It probably wasn't the best idea at the time, but it sure got her interested. She started asking questions about how I got Jimmy back into the mix, and how I finally got Ms. Griffin to agree to the cleaning.

"A lot of counseling. That's Jimmy's part."

"And your part is to get volunteers?"

"Yep, I really need help with this," I said. "I can't do this alone."

It was the same questions each time. The process was uncomfortable now, but I saw great things for Ms. Griffin in the future. We just needed to help her navigate through her stuff.

"A little trash and a little hard work never bothered me," Grandpa huffed when I asked him to help. I could always count on Grandpa when I needed him.

Grandma was a little bit harder to convince.

"There you go again, Allison," Grandma sighed. "I'm just not sure."

"Please, Grandma," I begged.

"Can I make a deal with you?" Grandma tapped me on the nose. "You've got to promise me that when this is over, you'll start going for things you want. Not just for things that other people want."

"What do you mean?"

"Stop trying to please everyone, Allison," Grandma laughed. "Deal?"

"Guess so," I sighed. "I just like seeing everyone happy."

"Not everyone will be happy," Grandma told me. "But it's nice to see you try."

I wasn't sure if I should have been discouraged, but her comments only stood like a challenge to me. They only made me want to work harder to finish this project.

"So you'll do it?"

"Of course," Grandma agreed.

I needed a different approach when asking Robyn and the others. I couldn't make it sound like work, it had to sound like fun.

"Guys?" I began sweetly. "Can I ask you all for a huge favor?"

"Cut it with the baby voice," Robyn poked me. "What do you need?"

"It's kind of a big deal, and I don't want you guys to freak out when I ask, okay?"

"Just ask us, Allison!" Audrey rolled her eyes.

"Alright here it goes," I sighed, "Would you guys be willing to spend a day cleaning out Ms. Griffin's clutter?"

"What?" Carter jumped. "Why?"

"Look, it's not that bad," I tried to ease the confusion that was smacked across each of their faces. "It'll be fun."

"Fun? How?" Robyn shook her head, "I'm not sure I want to go back in there."

"Yeah, Ms. Griffin is kind of weird," Rob agreed. "Besides, we have other fun things to do."

"Oh, come on!" I cried. "How would you like it if you had to live in a house filled with trash?" I tried to sound caring, but it came out rather harsh.

"Maybe she wouldn't have to live in a house filled with trash if she hadn't started hoarding in the first place," Audrey retorted.

I was lost for words. I couldn't understand how anyone could be so heartless, but I knew that I needed their help to get the job done. I had no one else to turn to for help, and I knew that I couldn't get the whole job done without more volunteers.

"Here, just listen," I began, forming a plan in my head that would make them want to help. "You wouldn't have to clean out the yucky stuff, only the interesting stuff. It'd be like going through the attic in Grandma's house, only it'd be in Ms. Griffin's bedrooms."

"Bedrooms?" Travis frowned. "I thought the stuff was only in the basement."

"I did too until she showed me the upstairs," I shrugged.

"So nothing gross?" Audrey started to warm up to the idea. "And it'd be fun?"

"Yes exactly!" I smiled. "It would fun. You just have to promise that you'll help."

"I promise," Travis laughed. "It's really cute that you care this much."

"I promise too," Carter agreed quickly. "It sounds like it wouldn't be so bad, I guess."

"Great!" I smiled. "How about you Audrey?"

"I don't know," Audrey mumbled.

"I'll do it if you do it," Rob nudged Audrey.

"Oh, alright," Audrey smiled sheepishly.

"And Robyn?" I looked at her hopelessly.

"No way," Robyn shook her head.

"Please? I'll make you in charge of the garage sale?" I tried to persuade her.

"Garage sale?" Robyn bit her lip. She loved selling things for a higher price than they were actually worth. "What's that for?"

"It's for all the stuff that we can re-sell," I told her. "The stuff we find that's worth something."

"What do you mean?"

"You'll just have to see what I mean when we start the process."

"Fine!" Robyn frowned. "I promise too."

CHAPTER EIGHTEEN

The next morning I quickly threw on a pair of old jeans and brushed my hair up into a messy bun.

"A granola bar for you," Grandma winked and handed me a granola bar. "I didn't want to waste time on making a big breakfast. Besides, I think I hear some of your little friends outside already."

I pressed my ear against the front door and waited for a knock.

"Are you sure?" I asked Grandma.

"Look out the window." Grandma suggested. Outside, Grandpa was lining up the twins next to Audrey and Carter. Robyn was talking to Aunt Stella, while each of them pulled sanitation gloves over their hands.

"They're waiting for me?" I gasped. "I thought I was up early!"

"They wanted to surprise you," Grandma giggled. "Act surprised when we get out there, okay?"

"Okay." I smiled. I ate up my granola bar and slipped on my shoes.

"Ready to go?" Grandma asked.

"Yep," I said. "Let's get to work."

Grandma grabbed the door knob and pulled gently. The sound of morning birds' chirps were drowned out by Grandma's giggles. She was having a bit of a hard time concealing her excitement.

"Surprise!" Carter yelled once the door was open.

"Carter!" Audrey hissed. "We weren't ready! We were going to do it on the count of three!"

"Too bad," Carter laughed with a smug grin smeared across his face. "Did I surprise you Allison?"

"Sure, Carter," I smiled. Out of the corner of my eye, I saw Jimmy pull into the driveway in his pickup truck. "Stay here everyone! I'll be right back."

"Hey Allison!" Jimmy yelled. "I have all the supplies." He waved me over and I hurried to meet him. "Help me unload them into the garage."

"Sure thing," I said, taking an armful of rubber sanitation gloves and a bottle of disinfecting spray. We talked about the plan as we unloaded the trash bags, work gloves and masks, cleaners, and bug sprays.

"Don't forget to look out for that watch my mom wanted," Jimmy reminded me. "I know it's really important to her."

"I'll remember," I promised Jimmy, though I'd forgotten all about it until he reminded me.

"Alright," He sighed. "I guess that's it." He handed me the key to the house and closed his truck door. "I'll take her once she's finished packing for the weekend."

With all the details locked in, I said goodbye to Jimmy and he made his way into the house to pick up Ms. Griffin.

"What's the plan, Allison?" Grandma asked me as I walked back to the group of volunteers gathered around the front lawn. Grandma was dressed in her work jeans, stained with blue paint and spaghetti sauce.

"Well, I guess the first thing we should do is divide up into different cleaning teams."

Grandma gathered the troops and I assigned everyone a position.

"Audrey, you'll be in charge of the upstairs bedrooms." I handed her a black trash bag and a whistle.

"Yay!" She gave me a thumbs-up. I knew that if I put her in charge, she'd be bossy enough to keep the work going. "What's the whistle for?"

"For blowing of course," Robyn answered for me and rolled her eyes.

"Robyn, you'll be in charge of organizing things for the garage sale."

"Sounds good," she said and took a clip board to record things she found.

"Grandma, Aunt Stella, and I will bring stuff outside where Grandpa will decide to throw it out or sell it at the garage sale." I finished up the jobs. Grandpa was always realistic about quick decisions, and I could count on him for getting the job done.

At around 8:45 a.m. Jimmy pulled his truck out of the driveway. I told my volunteers to wait in the backyard, because we didn't want Ms. Griffin to feel bad about having so many people in her cluttered house. I peeked around the side of the house and watched them go down the street. Ms. Griffin sat in the passenger seat and her overnight bags were thrown in the back of the truck. Jimmy honked the horn as he passed the house and I could see him wave as he drove away.

Once they left, everyone got right to work.

"What about me, Allison?" Carter frowned. "I want a special job too."

"Of course!" I laughed. "I have an important job just for you."

"Really? What is it?" Carter's eyes grew wide.

"I need you to find a watch."

"A watch?" Carter was slightly disappointed.

"Not just any watch, though," I clarified. "It's Ms. Griffin's watch. It has her wedding date engraved in the back. Are you up for the challenge?"

"Sure!" He beamed and ran inside the house.

At around 9:00 a.m. a truck carrying the dumpster arrived. Grandpa was in charge of throwing things away, so he instructed the driver where to put it. We needed it close to the house so we didn't have to walk far to throw things in it.

"How'd you get a dumpster, Allison? It's huge!" Grandma exclaimed.

"I guess Jimmy organized it." I was just as stunned. "He knew that we needed a way to get rid of all her stuff, but I didn't know he'd get one of these."

"He didn't," Aunt Stella giggled. "I did."

Grandma looked at her with confusion.

"What?" Aunt Stella laughed. "That's not the only surprise up my sleeve." She raised an eyebrow mysteriously. "You'll see."

Minutes after she spoke, the next delivery arrived.

"Some tables here!" A well-dressed man with a truck full of tables pulled into Ms. Griffin's driveway. He was slightly bald on the top of his head, and his few puffs of white hair that created a ring around his bald spot. He had a gray, long beard that flopped down to his shoulders.

"Oh perfect for the garage sale!" Aunt Stella smiled. She put down her latest haul from the basement and hurried over to the man. "Thanks Father Brian!"

"Father Brian?" Grandma gasped.

"Nice to see you off the weekend ma'am!" Father Brian smiled. "I'm here to drop off the tables you called for."

"From the church?" Grandma asked.

"The community of Saint Francis Church will also take any leftovers from the garage sale as donations for the homeless or poor." Father Brian unloaded the tables and jumped back in the car. "Return the tables anytime!" He called as he drove away. "Glad we could help!"

"You called the church?" Grandma laughed.

"Only because I knew that we needed tables for the garage sale and we could use them for free if we donated the extra garage sale stuff." Aunt Stella shrugged.

"You're more invested in this project than I thought you'd be, Aunt Stella," I said. "I thought you had bad memories of Jimmy."

"I did," Aunt Stella continued, "but Jimmy's proving to be a better son than I'd imagined him to be. I'm hoping that once this is over, Ms. Griffin will get more help for her problems."

"I know she will." I smiled. "Jimmy has already arranged for more counseling meetings with Dr. Hill."

"Good," Aunt Stella said.

"Was that the last of your surprise deliveries?"

"Not quite yet," she winked.

"What's all this?" Robyn poked her head out the bedroom window after hearing the commotion from Father Brian's delivery.

"How's it going up there?" I called back.

"Pretty good! You can come up in a little while," Robyn shouted. "What are those tables for?"

"The garage sale!"

"I'll be right down!" Robyn slammed the window shut.

We could hear her footsteps bouncing off each stair in Ms. Griffin's house. Her eyes were open wide, and her smile was as bright as the sun that was getting hotter with every minute that ticked by.

"I got this." Robyn pushed us aside and slammed down three rolls of duct tape and a stack of multi-color construction paper. "I'll label each table so it'll be easier to sell things."

"She's more organized than I am," Grandma laughed.

"Grandma?" Lexie cried, running out of our house crying. She hurried across our front lawn, still dressed in her purple fairy pajamas.

"Lexie, honey! Over here!" Grandma picked her up and gave her a kiss on the forehead. "I thought you were going to sleep in late."

Lexie tucked her head in Grandma's shoulder and kept her pink lips shut. Grandma rocked her for a few minutes and sighed.

"I'm going to take her over to the Fergus's house and see if Joshy's mom is willing to babysit for a few hours," Grandma told me.

"Here I come!" Audrey announced. She marched through Ms. Griffin's front door with two boxes piled in her thin, lanky arms. "Where should we put the first batch of things for the garage sale?"

"Ask Robyn, she's getting the tables set up over there." I pointed.

"Wow!" Aunt Stella smiled. "Things are going great, huh?" She dropped two small boxes in front of me and shook out her arms. "They're a bit numb, but I think it's all good."

"So far, so good!" Grandpa yelled from the top of the dumpster.

He pushed more of Ms. Griffin's castoffs to the back and clapped his calloused hands to get the dust off.

"This is just like gardening," he winked. "It's only fun once you've gotten a little stinky."

"Gross," Aunt Stella laughed.

I rolled the black and blue pen across my palm and calculated the number of trips I'd have to take to finish by lunch.

"We should probably speed up," I said, wiping my forehead free from the sweat that had built up in my pores. "There's too much stuff down there than people up here."

"Hmm," Aunt Stella giggled to herself and picked up another round of boxes. "Good thing more people are coming."

I was about to ask her what she meant, when an unfamiliar minivan jerked around the corner and into Ms. Griffin's driveway.

"Awesome!" Aunt Stella exclaimed and ran up to the window. She leaned her head in and motioned me to come over with her pointer finger. I hesitated, but eventually gave in.

"Is this the great Allison?" The driver had a hearty laugh and a thin shadow of a mustache. "We're at your command, ma'am."

"Wait," I paused and leaned in closer. "You're Charles!"

"Why, yes! Well, sort of," the driver laughed. "Charles was just a character I played at the theater."

"One of many," Aunt Stella murmured and rolled her eyes.

"My real name is Ian," he continued. "Ian Kirchner, at your service."

He stuck out his bulky, hairy hand through the open window and snatched my elbow. He wiggled it back and forth, slowly at first and then really fast.

"That's how I shake hands." Ian flashed a big white smile and leaned back in his seat. "Alright guys! Let's get to work."

"How many are there?" I whispered to Aunt Stella.

"I invited the whole theater troupe, but I'm not sure how many Ian could pile in his van," Aunt Stella whispered back. "My logic was that Ms. Griffin would be less embarrassed with strangers doing this kind of work than friends or family. These guys that work on the play set are strong, Allison. I'm pretty sure we can set up a chain of people in the basement to the dumpster so that it'd be less of a hassle to bring stuff up. We could get things going really fast. The faster we get this done, the more effective we'll be in the long run."

"You sound like Carter during the water battle," I laughed, "but I totally agree."

"I'll take them down to the basement so we can start working." Aunt Stella beamed.

About ten people tumbled out of Ian Kirchner's van. Most of them had facial hair of some sort, except for two because they were girls, and everyone had on a red and green t-shirt that read "Red Pen Theater Troupe – Revolutionary Group that Eats Vegetable Soup".

"Like our shirts?" One of the bearded men smirked.

"Alright guys!" Aunt Stella sang. "Let's get going!"

"On the farm, we've been living..." The Red Pen Theater Troupe started a song in perfect harmony. It was one of the songs from the play the other day. *"Many years we'd work, even though Thanksgiving..."*

"They like to sing while they work." Aunt Stella shrugged. "This happened all the time during rehearsal too. Don't worry, I'll tell them what to do."

"I guess you won't need my help?" I laughed and started to hum along to the familiar tune. "I should go check up on the upstairs and see how they're doing."

"Good idea." Aunt Stella nodded and led The Red Pens to the basement.

I went the opposite direction and climbed the rickety staircase up. The floorboards shook as my weight shifted between each foot.

"How's it going up here?" I called, but I got no reply. "Hello?" I knocked on the first bedroom door, where I saw Robyn, Audrey, and Rob head up earlier.

"Shh!" Robyn's voice behind the door shrieked.

"C'mon," I sighed. "We can't mess around right now."

"No, seriously, you're going to scare it," Robyn whispered back.

"It?"

"Yeah," Robyn said. "We found it about two minutes ago, and we think it's sleeping."

"Or dead," another voice said behind the door.

"Can I come in and see what it is?" I suggested.

"Okay, but don't be too loud."

I grabbed the brass door knob and pushed the door forward slowly.

"It's not opening," I whined.

"It's a pull, not a push," Robyn snickered.

"Oh, whoops," I brushed off my mistake. "Got it." I shoved the door open a crack and poked my head around the side.

"Do you see it?" Robyn murmured. She was up against the wall; her ear was about three inches away from the light switch that sat on the right side of the door. Audrey and Rob were huddled together on the floor next to Robyn.

"I don't see anything," I grimaced. "But I do smell something horrible. Gosh, what is that?" I plugged my nose and thrust the rest of my body through the door.

"That's why I think it's dead," Rob complained.

"Don't say that!" Audrey slapped his arm. "It might get offended."

"Where is it?" My voice sounded super nasally with my nose plugged to keep the smell out.

"Under there." Audrey pointed. "We were moving the plastic bags from under the bed and then we found it next to those two big boxes."

"Show me," I said.

"Not me." Audrey frowned. "I'm not going to get rabies today."

"I'll show you." Rob stood up. "I think it's dead."

He led me over the opposite side of the bed and leaned down to the floor.

"Do you see it?" He pointed between the gap of the floor and bed.

"Wait," I laughed. "This?"

I stuck my hand down and grabbed it.

"No!" Rob shrieked, but it was too late.

"Guys!" I shouted. "Calm down!"

"It's a gray beanie baby," Rob sighed after taking a better look at it.

"Seriously?" Audrey laughed. "That was probably the stupidest thing I've ever been scared of."

"Nah," Robyn nudged her as they recovered from their fear. "I think feet are the stupidest things you've ever been scared of."

"Not true," Audrey protested. "I've got lots of reasons to be scared of feet. You could get warts. It's just gross."

"Wait a second," Rob paused. "What made that horrible smell?"

"Sorry." Robyn rubbed her stomach slowly. "I get bad gas when I'm nervous."

"Now *that* is gross." Audrey took a step back and crinkled her nose.

I tossed the beanie baby on the bed and clapped my hands. "Now that I've solved that problem, how's it going up here?"

"Pretty good," Robyn smiled. "We got through the whole load on the bed, you remember. It's the stuff that Audrey brought down in those boxes."

"How's the yard sale part going?"

"Good too," Robyn nodded. "I don't know how Travis and Carter are doing though."

"I better go check on them next," I said. "By the way, The Red Pens are here to help. So if you see a bearded man, or many bearded men, don't get freaked out. They're helping in the basement."

"Cool," Rob smirked and rubbed his hairless face.

"I'll be back soon," I smiled and snuck out the door.

I turned and faced the second bedroom door. Before I knocked, I pressed my ear against the wooden door and listened.

There wasn't much noise coming from behind the door, just shuffles of feet and the sound of paper and plastic being rolled around.

"Hey! It's Allison." I knocked.

"Come on in," a voice was muffled behind the door.

"How's it going?" I asked as I walked in.

"Ask Carter." Travis rolled his eyes.

"Shut up, Travis." Carter frowned.

"What's going on?" I asked. "What's wrong?"

"Carter's just bossy." Travis ran a hand through his dark hair and picked up another bag. "We've been working in silence."

"Only because you weren't getting anything done!" Carter accused.

"I was just trying to make conversation!" Travis yelled back.

"Guys chill!" I said. "This is supposed to be fun."

"I'm not having any fun," Carter moaned. "It'd be more fun if you were in here instead of Travis."

"Same goes for me," Travis dropped his bag and headed for the door.

"Don't go!" I begged.

"I'm not leaving," Travis said. "I'm just going to help out in the other room."

"Please don't, they've just had an episode and they're still recovering. Besides, it smells awful." I said. Travis cracked a smile, but shook his head.

"We've got a lot done," Travis said. "Maybe it'd be best if we took a break and cooled off."

"Good idea." I smiled. "Do you want me to take some of the stuff that you've sorted down to the garage sale tables?"

"I got it," Carter said. "I want to see what's going on in the basement anyway."

"Don't disrupt The Red Pens," I told him as he left the room with a pile of items for the garage sale.

"The Red Pen Theater Troupe?"

"Yeah, Aunt Stella called them to help out with the basement. There's a lot of heavy stuff down there that Grandma and Aunt Stella couldn't lift on their own."

"Okay, I won't bother them," Carter said and trudged down stairs.

"Why can't you guys just get along?" I turned to Travis.

"It's just how we work, I guess," Travis shrugged. "He likes plans and order while I'd rather have fun with it."

"Hmm," I glanced around the room. "There is still a lot of stuff in here."

"I know," Travis frowned.

"How about I work up here with you guys too?" I offered. "And I'll see if any of the others would want to help in here for a little bit. Maybe you and Carter can sort out your problems while we work?"

"I'm willing," Travis said. "It's not really Carter's fault. I just get so overwhelmed with cleaning. Especially with all this stuff..." he trailed off and stuck his fists against his hips and shook his head. "There's just so much. It makes me remember our old foster parents."

"Just think of Ms. Griffin," I dug into a pile of untouched plastic bags and pulled out teddy bear. "Do you think this looks alright to sell at the garage sale?"

"Yeah, I guess so," Travis shrugged. "Why are you always so positive, Allison?"

"I'm optimistic." I smiled and handed him the teddy bear. "I'm optimistic that we can get this done."

"Me too." He smiled back and took a seat on the bed. "I'll start to sort through these and you can get the others."

"Us?" Audrey beamed and pushed the door open with her foot. "We just took down the next bunch, Allison."

"Great," I said.

"Do you need us up here?" Audrey smirked. "Doesn't look like there's been much progress. I bet it was Carter, huh?" She nudged Travis and winked.

"Nah, it was me too," Travis sighed. "Do you want to help out?"

"Sure!" Audrey grinned. "I'll get Robyn and Rob."

"Robyn and Rob," Travis laughed. "I've never heard their names together before."

"It sounds like they've got the same name."

"Sort of," Travis's dimples formed a frame around his cheeks. "Only Rob's full name is Robert, not Robyn."

"Don't tell them my full name!" Rob snapped as he joined the conversation.

"Why?" Audrey giggled.

"He thinks it sounds stuffy," Travis explained.

"Come on in guys!" I waved them in. The doorway was crowding up and it was making me feel uncomfortable.

"I checked all the tables for the garage sale." Robyn took a seat next to me on the crowded bed and pushed some plastic bags to the ground. "It's going great, but the tables might get a little crowded once we finish up in here."

"Don't worry about it." Carter wandered into the room with two bags of Doritos. "I know someone who'd buy half the stuff on the tables. Well, mostly those model cars and baseball gear."

"Let me guess, you?" Audrey rolled her eyes.

"Where did you get those Doritos?" Rob licked his lips.

"Why? You want some?" Carter laughed and threw a bag at him. "I got one from those singing guys with beards."

"The Red Pens?" I smiled. "They're awesome aren't they?"

"Totally," Carter mumbled, his mouth painted with red, Dorito-flavored dust.

"Come on, let's start working on all the stuff you guys haven't sorted through." Audrey snapped her fingers and snatched up a plastic bag with a square tag dangling from the side. "Come on guys!"

"Calm down," Robyn rolled over on her belly. "Looks like a skirt." She said pointing to Audrey's bag.

"Get motivated!" Audrey shouted and kicked the frame of the bed.

"Hey!" Robyn moaned and rolled over again.

"Audrey's right." Travis stood, "We can't let those singing guys with beards beat us in the motivation category."

"Then what do you propose we do about it?" Carter slurred, sticking his hand down the Dorito bag for more chips.

"We sing, of course!" Audrey chimed. "If they're singing keeps them going, why can't our singing keep us going?"

"Not exactly what I was going for," Travis grimaced.

"Hmm," Robyn yawned. "I'm not sure that's the best way to go about motivation. I'm not much of a singer."

"I guess giving you a position of power was a bad move on my part," I shrugged.

"What do you mean?" Robyn frowned. "I've done all my work."

"I should've known not to expect things from you." I breathed in deep.

"I see what you're doing," Audrey whispered.

"Come on, Allison!" Robyn scowled and sat up. "I can be full of motivation!"

"Prove it." Audrey raised her eyebrows and tossed the bag she was holding straight on Robyn's lap.

"Alright, I will." Robyn accepted the challenge and started digging in the bag. "See! A skirt." She lifted the black laced skirt out of the bag slowly.

"Hold on a second," Carter wiped his mouth with his Dorito-free hand and reached for the skirt.

"Stop that!" Robyn slapped his hand away. "You still have that red stuff all over your hand!"

Carter wiped his hand on his blue jeans and dropped his Dorito bag to the floor.

"Better?" He asked sarcastically.

"I still don't want you to touch this skirt," Robyn said. "We can sell this at the garage sale. It still has a price tag on it."

"I don't need the skirt. I need this." Carter reached again for the plastic bag, but Robyn shuffled away. "Seriously, Robyn?"

"Go wash your hands first," Robyn ordered.

"Come on!" Carter rolled his eyes.

"Just let him see it," Travis shrugged. "We can always wash the skirt before the garage sale."

"Fine," Robyn pouted.

Carter snatched it away from her and stuck his face deep into the fabric of the skirt, taking in one deep breath before returning.

"I knew it," He smirked and reached his red hand into the bag and through the skirt. "It must have slipped off her wrist when she bought this skirt."

Out came a silvery white, diamond–incrusted, watch. Time had frozen as the hands rusted against the black numbers, and parts of the glass had chipped away from neglect.

"Ms. Griffin's watch!" I exclaimed and extended my hand to hold it.

"I thought so, but I wasn't sure," Carter examined the watch closely and nudged my hand away with his elbow.

"You've got to keep it safe," I told him. "Don't let it get mixed up with stuff from the garage sale."

"I won't," Carter flashed me a smile. "Look here."

He flipped the watch upside-down and pointed to the gold circle in the middle of the back.

Every moment with you, is a moment of time cherished. August 14, 1970

"Oh," My heart started to swell. "No wonder she wanted to save that so much."

"Yeah," Carter sniffed. "I'll keep it safe." He slipped the watch into his pocket and continued wiping his hands on his pants. "This stuff never comes off, does it?"

"You gotta lick it," Rob laughed and licked his pointer finger, "and then stick it into someone's ear."

"Don't you dare." Audrey's eyes grew wide.

"I wasn't going for you," Rob laughed and wiped the saliva on his sleeve.

"Are we going to work, or what?" Travis raised his eyebrows and sighed deeply. "I don't know about the rest of you, but I'd love to be done with this before it gets too late."

"Me too," Robyn agreed. She threw a Walmart plastic bag in my face. "Move it!"

"That's more like it!" I smiled.

****

We worked through the things around the flower patterned bed and across the cream colored carpeting for about three hours; finally achieving the progress we needed.

"Pretty good, huh?" Travis wiped some dust that gathered in the creases of his hands on the bed spread.

"This room was dirtier than the other one," Audrey complained. "Full of dust and dirt. Jeez, I have to wash my hands...arms... face..."

"Just think of it this way," Robyn smiled. "We just completed a task Ms. Griffin couldn't do in like ten years!"

"Kids!" Grandma's voice broke through the sound of endless footsteps from The Red Pens and the rustling of plastic bags. "Come on down for lunch! Jimmy had pizza delivered!"

"Let's carry everything that's trash down in those boxes and everything that's for the garage sale in those trash bags," Carter offered.

"No loser!" Rob laughed. "Carry everything that's trash in the trash bags and everything that's for the garage sale in the boxes. It's less confusing that way."

"Whatever works," I said. "Just make sure that the watch stays separate."

"Of course." Carter shot me a thumbs up and started piling the things to sell in the boxes.

"While you guys do that, I'm going to check and see what The Red Pens are doing," I told them.

"Still singing." Robyn rolled her eyes.

"I mean their progress," I said. "I have to make sure everything is sorted through on time."

"It's only like 1 o'clock, Allison," Travis laughed. "I'm sure we'll get everything done by tonight."

"Still," I sighed. "I'll see you guys down stairs for lunch, okay?" I inched the door open and snuck down the dense staircase.

"How's it going upstairs?" Aunt Stella's hair was wrapped up into two thick, disheveled buns.

"Pretty good." I smiled. "How're The Red Pens?"

"Magnificent, as always," she giggled. "But my voice is starting to get sore, especially when we sing the opening number to *Hairspray*."

"I bet pizza will do the trick!" Grandma called. "Come out girls! We're eating on the grass."

"So what's the plan for tomorrow?" Aunt Stella asked me, following Grandma's voice and the smell of pepperoni pizza.

"The final things," I said. "Like actually vacuuming and scrubbing the places where the stuff was removed."

"And the garage sale?"

"That'll be on Sunday, not tomorrow," I told her. "At least, that's when Robyn is planning on having it."

"When's Ms. Griffin coming back home?"

"Sunday afternoon," I said. "I really hope she's having a good time with her grandchildren, and that she's not worrying about her things."

"Allison, can I tell you something?" Aunt Stella said. "I think when you know that you're surrounded with people that love you unconditionally, all other problems kind of fade away. I bet Ms. Griffin doesn't even remember she owns a thing at all."

CHAPTER NINETEEN

"How's everything going?" Jimmy called early on Saturday morning.

"Pretty good, I think," I said, yawning. The sun was shining bright light through the thin fabric of the window curtains, warming up the cold phone against my cheek. "Aunt Stella's Red Pen Theater Troupe is coming back this morning to finish up the stuff in the basement. Then we've got to clean everything out."

"What do you mean?"

"It's mostly just dirt now. We've moved most of the big things out,"

"Great," I could hear a smile forming on the other end of the line. "Thanks again, Allison."

"Happy to help out," I said. "I better get going though. I need to get dressed before work starts."

"It's 8 in the morning," Jimmy laughed. "Pretty early isn't it?"

"A little bit," I shrugged and rubbed my eyes. My whole body felt drowsy and sluggish. It was still paralyzed with a want to sleep, even though I'd been awake for thirty minutes.

"Well, good luck," Jimmy said. His voice became cloaked with static as the reception died off the call.

"Who was that?" Robyn hopped into the room. She already was dressed in her blue overalls and wrinkled t-shirt as she slipped on her sneakers.

"Jimmy," I said, sliding off the counter stool. "He just wanted to check in."

"Makes sense," Robyn said. "Are you ready to go out?"

"Sure," I said. "Let me just throw on some clothes first."

"And fix your hair," Robyn murmured.

"Could you be any more direct?" I laughed. "I'll be quick."

"I think Audrey and Carter are already outside," Robyn said, peering through the kitchen window. "Want me to wait for you?"

"Nah, go ahead," I said.

"Thanks." Robyn smiled and slipped on her graying shoes. Like most things in the summer, they started out white.

"Is that from yesterday?" I asked. Robyn examined the fraying end of her laces and muttered something under her breath.

"It's from all the dust," She stood up and leaned against the pale painted door. "Can I ask you something, Allison?"

"Sure," I said.

"Why are we doing this?" Robyn asked bluntly.

"What do you mean?"

"Why are we helping Ms. Griffin? It's not like she's ever done anything for us."

"She has, but you just don't realize it," I whispered and slipped on my jacket. "I mean, I didn't even realize it until recently too. You know, until I connected the dots."

"Huh?" Robyn looked confused.

"Who do you think has been leaving us presents in the treehouse these past couple of days?" I nudged her. "C'mon. Didn't you realize that they stopped when she was gone?"

"Well I-I…" Robyn mumbled. "I didn't mean it in a negative way."

"I know, Robyn," I smiled. "Just don't be too quick to judge people. Ms. Griffin has a good heart, but it's a heart that has been stuffed with things that produced artificial love. I know she wants to change. We're putting family back into her life."

"Are you guys coming?" Carter yelled through the window. "We're going to get a head start before the Red Pen Theatre Troupe comes back."

"They're coming back?" Robyn turned to me.

"Yeah, they're going to help with the cleaning now that everything is moved out," I told her. "They're such nice guys."

"With great facial hair," she winked.

As we snuck out the front door, I could hear Grandpa and Grandma shuffle down the stairs. Grandpa and Grandma would be cutting Ms. Griffin's front lawn and trimming up the flower beds that had grown as crowded as Ms. Griffin's basement. Aunt Stella would be in the basement and around the house, managing the cleaning efforts.

Ian Kirchner and The Red Pen Theatre Troupe arrived early, before Aunt Stella had even woken up.

"We'll go sing to her and wake her up," Ian suggested.

"No need!" Aunt Stella yelled out of her bedroom window. "I'll be down in a few minutes!"

"Anyways," Ian winked. "What should we help with today, Miss Allison?"

"I believe we're cleaning up the house today," I said, "to get rid of the dust and dirt."

"Sounds splendid," another member of The Red Pen Theatre Troupe said. "And what musical would you like to hear today?"

"Sing the farm songs!" Robyn yelled.

"Alright, fellas! You heard the lady," Ian snapped. "One, two, three!"

"On the farm, we've been living..." They began. *"Many years we'd work, even though Thanksgiving..."*

"Oh, Allison!" Grandma pulled me aside. "Joshy and Lexie will be over today too."

"What? Why?" I asked.

"Joshy's mom will be out today, she got called into work," Grandma said. "And usually I'd just watch them back at our house, but I know we're working today. I promise you they won't get in the way."

"I'm not worried." I smiled. "I bet it'd be nice to have them over here."

"Good, good," Grandma said. "I'll be right back."

"Are you going to get them?"

"Yes, I'm going to wake Lexie up now," Grandma told me. "Joshy will be over when his mom drops him off."

"Sounds good," I said and headed upstairs to see Travis and Carter's cleaning progress.

"Guys! Listen to me!" I could hear Audrey shouting as I climbed the stairs. "I was put in charge, so you need to listen to me!"

"Oh boy," I sighed.

"We *are* listening to you, Audrey!" Carter shouted back. "Hey! Allison!" He hurried over to me and gave me a hug. "You always come at the most *desperate* of times."

"Don't get dramatic," I laughed. "What's going on?"

"Audrey is being bossy," Travis said. "What is it with you Fergus's?"

"Don't be rude," Audrey frowned. "You and you're brother are no picnic either."

"I thought we were friends!" Rob pouted.

"Guys!" I intervened. "Calm down!"

"Sorry," Audrey whispered to Rob. "I didn't mean to get bossy."

"At least you're apologizing, that's new." Carter rolled his eyes. "What's up Allison?"

"Joshy and Lexie will be over soon," I told them.

"Ugh, really?" Carter sighed. "Joshy is so annoying."

"So is Lexie," Robyn agreed. "They're too little to hang out with us."

"Well, like it or not, they'll be over soon," I said.

171

"Oh yeah," Audrey remembered. "My mom got called into work today."

"Anyways," I said. "Let's just finish with the cleaning quickly so we can play with Joshy and Lexie."

"Do we have to play with them?"

"I just feel like we should keep them distracted while Grandma and Grandpa fix up Ms. Griffin's yard." I said.

"I'm only playing with them until lunch," Audrey said.

"Don't make a big deal about it," I said. "Soon they'll play with us all the time."

"Why?"

"They're going to grow up!" I laughed. "And we're going to grow up too."

"Yeah, but for now, let's not grow up," Carter said. "I'm going to see if the bearded guys have any more Doritos."

"Wait!" I called to him. "Do you still have the watch?"

"Yep," Carter nodded and tapped his hip. "I got it right here in my pocket."

"Great," I sighed. "Let's start cleaning."

"I better get a bag of Doritos as a reward for all this cleaning," Rob mumbled. "I like Doritos, but I hate cleaning."

"It'll be over fast, I swear." I smiled.

"Allison!" Grandma called to me from the stairs. "Joshy's mom just dropped him off! Can you take him upstairs with you?"

Audrey moaned.

"Lexie is here too!"

Robyn moaned.

"That's fine!" I said and went to meet Grandma at the bottom of the staircase. "I'll take them upstairs."

"Great, thanks Allison," Grandma said. She was covered in grass snippets and her short hair was stuck to her sweaty forehead.

"Is everything going okay?" I asked.

"Just a lot of work, honey," Grandma said and pinched my cheeks with her gardening gloves.

I took Lexie and Joshy's hands and helped them up the staircase.

"Where are we going?" Joshy mumbled as he tripped on the last stair.

"Are you okay?" I giggled at his little grumpy reaction. "We're going to play up here for a little while."

The others were sitting in the first room on a floral bedspread they'd set out on the floor. Carter had returned with a sack of Doritos for everyone.

"We're taking a Dorito break," Carter explained. "You can bring Joshy and Lexie over here."

"Does that sound okay?" I asked the two little toddlers. Neither of them answered, but Lexie nodded.

"Want some Doritos?" Carter asked Joshy.

"Please," he whispered.

"Aw, he's so cute!" Robyn laughed. "How about you, Lexie?"

"No thank you," She said. "I wanna play."

"Spoiled brat," Robyn muttered. "There are no toys here. We just cleaned it all out."

"All the toys?" Lexie asked sadly.

"No, there were all kinds of stuff," Robyn told her.

"Maybe we could find something for them to play with," Audrey suggested. "So they can be distracted while we work."

"What could we give them?" Travis asked.

Carter slipped the precious watch out of his pocket and dangled it in front of Joshy.

"Don't you dare." I glared at him.

"I'm not going to!" Carter insisted. "I was only messing with him."

"Be careful, Carter," Rob said. "He's going to want it if you show him."

"He's my brother, Rob." Carter rolled his eyes and stuck the watch back in his pocket.

"Finish up your Doritos," Audrey said. "I want to be done with cleaning so Robyn and I can work on the garage sale."

"Can we not clean and say we did?" Carter flopped on his back.

"You wish," Robyn laughed. "We'll take the second room. C'mon Audrey!"

"I'll go with you," I said and stood up.

"Alright, but you're doing the gross cleaning," Robyn said.

"You guys will need to watch the little ones," I said. "Can you do it? Or should I bring them with me?"

"No problem!" Carter said. "I watch Joshy all the time at home."

"No he doesn't," Audrey whispered to me.

I followed Audrey into the second bedroom and picked up a broom that Grandpa had brought up for us to use.

"Those boys will only make their room dirtier," Audrey said. "I bet if we went back in there, the room would be painted red from Dorito dust."

"Focus on this room, Audrey," Robyn said. "I want to spend more time on the garage sale."

"Want to listen to some music while we clean?" I suggested. "That always makes time go by faster when I do chores back home."

"Sure!" Audrey smiled. "Got any good boy band groups?"

"Um," I checked. "Yep, I got tons of boy band songs."

"Oh, I just love boy bands," Robyn mocked me.

"Whatever, Robyn," I said. "I'm just going to put it on shuffle, okay Audrey?"

"Yay!" She cheered and began to sing along.

Cleaning with Robyn and Audrey was fun. Almost like a musical, we sang in perfect harmony and we almost had the cleaning done within an hour.

"You guys stay here," I said in between songs. "I'm going to check on the boys."

"My favorite song just started!" Audrey giggled and started to dance along with the music.

""Be back soon," Robyn said to me. "We've got to take these sheets down to the washing machine."

"Okay, I'll be quick," I said.

I whipped around the corner and walked across the hall to the other room.

"Go fish," Rob said. He had three packs of cards in his lap and he was hunched over a set of three ace of spades. "I'm so close!"

"Allison!" Carter cheered. "We finished cleaning a few minutes ago."

"Wow nice job!" I said. The room looked immaculate, no dust bunnies under the bed or cobwebs in the corner. "How'd you get it done so fast?"

"Easy, just work together." Travis smiled. "We also kinda had a race to see who could get the most cleaned the fastest, so that probably helped."

"Yeah, I think so," I said. "Where did you get those cards?"

"We found them," Rob said. "When we stripped the bed of those dirty sheets, we found them wedged together in the covers."

"Oh yeah, and look here," Travis picked up one box of cards. "On the back it says Jimmy Griffin." He pointed to the light pen marks that must have been written by someone just learning their letters.

"You can barely read it," I laughed. "I've got to show Jimmy, though."

"Of course!" Travis said. "That's why we saved them and didn't put them down with the garage sale stuff."

"Are you guys done in the other room?" Carter asked.

"Not yet," I said. "But we're having a lot of fun too."

"Awesome," Rob said. "Can I go see Audrey? I want to show her a card trick."

"Sure," I said.

Rob hurried out of the room with a handful of cards.

"Are Joshy and Lexie hiding?" I asked.

"Um, no." Carter looked confused. "They followed you girls out when you left."

"Aren't they in your room?" Travis asked.

"What?" I froze. "Are they gone?"

"We thought they were with you!" Travis slapped his forehead.

"Oh gosh." Carter looked sick. "We've got to find them! I gave Joshy my last bag of Doritos!"

"And you're mom is going to be super angry when she finds out you lost your brother!" I gasped.

"*You* lost my brother!" Carter said.

"Well, we both need to find them," I said. "Because either way we'd both get in trouble."

"It can't be too hard." Travis tried to persuade himself. "I mean, now that all the stuff is gone, they've got to be out in the open."

"Maybe Grandma has them," I said. "But I really hope not."

"Why?" Carter exclaimed.

"Because then she'd know I failed at watching them," I frowned. I kneeled down and looked under the bed.

"Hm," Travis started pacing. "Think of all the places two three year olds could fit in."

"The kitchen," Carter said. "My brother loves food."

"We'd have to go past the basement entrance where The Red Pen Theatre Troupe is cleaning," I said, "Let's go."

I followed Travis and Carter down the stairs. We tried to stay quiet, because we didn't want to interrupt the bearded guys' song.

"Try to pass them during a chorus," Travis said. "If we don't want to be noticed, then the chorus is when the singing would be the loudest."

"Sounds good," I said.

"Those pesky babies," Carter mumbled. "I knew we shouldn't have agreed to watch them."

"It's too late to worry about what we should or shouldn't do," Travis explained. "By the way, Carter, do you still have that watch Allison wanted you to keep safe."

"Yeah it's right here in my pocket," Carter reached into his deflated pocket. He spent a good thirty seconds rummaging around. "Wait, maybe it's in this one," He laughed hesitantly as he search through his pants' pockets. "Oh gosh." He gulped and looked up at me slowly.

"Seriously, Carter?" I shrieked. "You lost the babies and now you lost the one thing that Ms. Griffin wanted?"

Travis smirked.

"Don't be happy about this!" I snapped.

"They're about to start a new song," Travis said. "Let's go now before they see us."

"I'm so sorry, Allison." Carter tugged on my arm. "I promise I'll find it."

"Sure, okay." I rolled my eyes. I was so angry and I just couldn't stand his apology.

"Hey kids!" Grandma called to us, just as we took off from the stairs. "Over here, Allison!"

"Darn," Travis sighed. "She caught us."

"Hi Grandma," I cringed.

"Is everything going okay?" She asked us.

"Yep, everything's great." I lied. "We were just heading back upstairs, right guys?"

"Yeah, right," Travis chimed in. "I guess we just like to hear the bearded guys sing a little."

"Oh, me too," Grandma smiled. "We're almost done gardening, so I'm going to prepare some lunch."

"Perfect," I said, pulling Carter and Travis up the stairs while Grandma turned away. "Bye, Grandma!"

"I'll call you down in 15 minutes, okay?" She called up the stairs.

"Okay!" We shouted back.

"Not okay!" Carter started to freak out. "This is not good at all! What are we going to do?"

"I'm not sure." I bit my lip. "I just don't know what to say."

Carter leaned against the closet door next to the room Audrey and Robyn were still working in and slowly sank to the floor.

"After all this work," I muttered.

"Wait," Carter paused.

Travis was about to say something, but Carter jumped up and slapped his hand over his mouth.

"Do you hear that?" Carter's eyes widened and he paused a moment to press his ear against the door.

"No, what is it?" I whispered.

"Come here," Carter smiled. "I think I found what we're looking for."

He plopped down on the ground and pulled Travis down with him. I kneeled down to meet them, but Carter kept getting lower.

"Put your ear right here." He pointed to the closet door.

I cautiously placed my ear where he was pointing and held my breath.

Tick, Tick, Tick, Tick

"It sounds like the crocodile from Peter Pan," I murmured. "But the watch you found didn't work, remember Carter? It couldn't be the same watch."

"It's not," Carter said. "But look here."

He shot the door open with one pull and pointed under the coats.

"Joshy! Lexie!" I cried. "Oh, thank goodness!"

"Wait, how did you know it was Joshy and Lexie?" Travis rubbed the area where Carter had slapped him and kneeled down to pick up the toddlers.

"Joshy has been making clock noises ever since we bought a cuckoo clock for his bedroom." Carter grinned. "See? You should be thanking me."

"You still lost the watch," Travis pointed out.

I picked up Lexie and gave her a big kiss on the cheek.

"Sissy!" She giggled and wrapped her arms around my neck.

"I was worried about you, Lexie," I told her. "Why did you run away?"

"I didn't, I followed Joshy," she said.

"You don't always need to follow Joshy," I laughed.

We took them into Audrey and Robyn's room and placed them on the bare mattress. They started to bounce a little, and it made me think of last summer when we took them on the trampoline for the first time. They didn't like it very much, but they'd grown so much since then.

"They're going to be like us someday," I said to Carter. "Next summer we should teach them Wolf."

"Yeah," Travis interrupted. "But this summer we need to find that watch."

"Allison, you never came back." Robyn poked me. "We had to finish the cleaning without you."

"Luckily Rob was in here to help out," Audrey smiled. "Did you guys say you lost Ms. Griffin's watch?"

"This watch?" Rob asked. I had almost forgotten that he was in here with Audrey and Robyn. "I was using it for my magic trick. No harm done."

"Sweet!" Carter grabbed it from him. "Now I don't have to feel guilty anymore."

"How'd you get that?" I asked Rob.

"I took it from Carter's pocket while he wasn't looking," He whispered. "I'm a bit of a pickpocket when I need to be."

"Well, thank goodness you returned it," I smiled.

"The music stopped playing." Audrey handed me the iPod. "Can you make it play again."

"It's dead," I sighed. "No worries, I'll charge it during lunch."

"Oh lunch!" Robyn smiled. "I'm so hungry!"

"Good thing," I said. "Grandma is going to call us any minute."

I needed to take a break and rest on the bed. So much had happened so quickly, it was hard to absorb everything. Lost the twins, lost the watch. Found the twins, found the watch.

"You okay?" Travis asked, taking a seat next to me. "A bit exciting, isn't it?"

"What's exciting?" I asked, a little bit out of it and a little bit tired.

"We finished," he said. "The house is clean. No more stuff."

"Oh my gosh." I took a second and thought about all the work we'd done in the past two days. "You're right."

"Kids! Lunch!" Grandma shouted up the stairs. Travis and I picked up the toddlers and followed the others down the stairs.

"The dumpster is being picked up at 5 tonight, too," Travis smiled at me. "The junk will be gone forever."

CHAPTER TWENTY

"Garage sale day!" Robyn's shouting woke me up at six the next morning. "I've got everything planned out! It's going to be great!"

"Yeah," I yawned and rubbed my tired, morning eyes. "I believe you, Robyn."

"Whose coming back to help on the garage sale?" Robyn asked me. "Will The Red Pens come back?"

"Unfortunately," I sighed. "I don't think they'll be able to make it a third day."

"Darn," Robyn said. "I was really starting to like their beards."

"Me too," I laughed.

Robyn and I hurried downstairs for breakfast,

"Oh Robyn," Grandma bumped into us in the hallway. "Just the girl I wanted to talk to."

"Hi Grandma, what's for breakfast?" Robyn smiled and snuck around to the kitchen.

"Well that's just the question," Grandma said. "What time are you opening up the garage sale?"

"I was thinking around seven," Robyn said, taking her favorite place at the table. "I'd need to go and put up a sign too, so that people would stop by."

"Good idea," Grandma said.

"What has that got to do with breakfast?"

"I haven't started breakfast, so I was thinking you and Allison could go put up some signs right now if you already have them made," Grandma said. "I'll have breakfast made by the time you get back."

"Okay, sounds like fun!" Robyn said.

"Grandpa and Aunt Stella can go with you two if you'd like," Grandma suggested.

"Nah, I think we got it," Robyn said and picked up the stack of signs she colored last night. "I wouldn't want to wake them up. I know how Grandpa is about sleeping in on Sundays." She grabbed her backpack full of supplies while I slipped on my sneakers and jacket.

"Ready to go?" I asked her. It was kinda fun working with Robyn. We hadn't spent a lot of time with just the two of us all summer, so putting up signs and getting ready for the garage sale would be fun to do with her.

"Yeah, I think so," she said. "Can you carry some of these?"

"Sure," I said, taking a handful of signs and roll of tape. "Where do you want to put them?"

"Follow me," she smiled. She hopped off the front porch and started sprinting down the street.

"Wait for me!" I shouted and ran to catch up with her. She was fast, but I was faster.

"I'm thinking of putting these up on the intersection that we pass when we drive down this street." She huffed, almost out of breath. "It's a little bit in the distance, but we can run and make it back on time for breakfast."

"Why so far?"

"The intersection is a busy place during the day, so a lot of cars would see it when they passed," Robyn explained. "The intersection is right down the street from that church. When people drive home, they might see these signs and think about taking a little detour. I really want this to be a success."

"Okay," I said and we carried on running without talking for a while.

We made it to the end of our grandparent's street and we took a left. Soon we'd made it to the main intersection that was visited daily by commuters and soccer moms.

"Okay," Robyn said and wiped the sweat from her forehead. "I'll put some up on the other side. You can put those up on this side."

"Be careful crossing the street," I said.

"I will," she said and hurried across the empty street.

I took out the signs and pulled out the roll of tape from my pocket. I stuck up three signs on the cross-walk pole, once facing each direction that a car could see it. I glanced over to Robyn, to make sure I was doing it right.

Robyn was standing on her tiptoes to reach the same height I had reached without my tiptoes. She gestured a thumbs up and ran back over to meet me.

"Good?" I asked, showing her what I'd done.

"Perfect," she smiled. "I'm so excited!"

"Me too," I said. "I'll race you back?"

"Deal," she said and started off sprinting.

Naturally, I won.

"No fair." She was out of breath by the time she got home. I was already inside, drinking my second glass of water. "You've got longer legs than me."

"True," I breathed, "but I still won."

"Oh, you girls are back early!" Grandma said. She was just finishing up a stack of pancakes and a side of fruit salad. "Can you go get Lexie, Robyn?"

"Sure thing." Robyn was still exhausted.

I helped Grandma set the table and put the food out for everyone. We always had a big breakfast on Sundays.

"So this is it," Grandma smiled at me. "Now you know I'm not always fond of you meddling in other people's business, but I have to say, this one really paid off. I think Ms. Griffin is going to be much more comfortable when she gets home."

"I'm a little worried," I told Grandma. "What if she's not? What is she misses her stuff so much that it drives her into an even harder addiction?"

"That's doubtful, Allison." Grandma gave me a hug. "She's receiving more help. Counseling will be useful and effective."

"I just hope you're right."

"What time does she get back?"

"This afternoon," I smiled. "Jimmy's thinking around four. That way we'll have time to clean up the garage sale too. We don't want her to worry about anything. The money will be a nice extra thing, like a present."

"How sweet!" Grandma smiled. "I'm going to wake up Grandpa and Stella."

"Alright," I said and took a seat at the kitchen table. I thumbed through some of Grandma's recipe books while I waited, and I found one titled Extra Pink Strawberry Shortcake. I thought it looked yummy so I turned the page. On the top corner it said Beth Griffin.

"Oh that was Ms. Griffin's old recipe," Grandma saw me looking at it as she came back into the kitchen, followed by a sleepy Aunt Stella. "I used it for Easter one year. You know, Beth loves to bake."

I could hear the door open quickly and then shut with a loud slam.

"Robyn's going to organize the tables," Grandma explained like she read my mind.

"Can I go out and help her?" I asked. "I'll take my breakfast to go?"

"Just eat something really quick," Grandma insisted.

"Fine," I moaned and ate three pancakes.

"Honey," Grandpa kissed Grandma on the cheek and took a seat next to Aunt Stella. "Not awake either?"

"Not one little bit." Aunt Stella stretched her arms out across the table.

"All this work you've put us through has been tiresome, Allison," Grandpa yawned. "But we're glad to help out with your little project."

"Thanks," I smiled. "I'm glad you could help out too."

"How's that book going?"

That book. Ever since I'd started on the Ms. Griffin project, my mind's been too full to even remember my whole plan for the summer. I was going to write a book about my adventures with my friends, and I'd spent all this time figuring out mysteries and organizing clean-ups instead of taking notes.

"It'll happen someday," I told Grandpa. "I guess you're right, though."

"I'm right?" Grandpa looked a little confused. "That's a first."

"No, I'm serious." I shrugged. "I guess I just couldn't write a book this summer. Maybe when I'm older."

"Allison," Grandpa frowned. "You're the hardest worker I know. When you set your sights on helping Ms. Griffin, you didn't stop for a second. You've honestly set her straight in life. Gosh, you've even rekindled her relationship with her son! I'm certain that you can do anything if you really want to."

"I hope you're right, Grandpa," I smiled. "It's just that right now my mind is set on the garage sale."

"Then get out there." Grandpa patted me on my back.

"Go ahead." Grandma nodded and excused me from the breakfast table.

I rushed out the front door to meet Robyn at the garage sale area that was being set up in the driveway.

"Grandma let you go outside?" Robyn laughed and pointed in the distance. "The twins are coming."

"So that just leaves Audrey and Carter as the two sleepy heads." I smirked.

"Who you calling a sleepy head?" Audrey poked me with a hanger she had in her hand. "We've been out here for like five minutes."

"Allison!" Carter called when he saw me. He pulled me over to the tables he was responsible for organizing to show me his display. We were trying to make the garage sale look as appealing and delightful as a professional business. "How does this look?"

"It looks great," I smiled. "I better go start my part."

"You're going to be sorting through the books because you like words, right?" Robyn pointed to the two tables in the front. "She's got a lot of books."

"Great, that seems easy enough," I said. Carter was sorting through dishes and silverware, Audrey was setting up the skirts and jackets on hangers, and Robyn was checking off things on her notepad. The twins arrived minutes after I finished setting up the first table of books.

"What'cha working on Allison?" Travis asked me.

"Setting up the books," I said. "I think Robyn's got some jobs for you guys. I'd go now before she gets in a bad mood."

"Good idea," He laughed and went to Robyn for his job assignment.

"Everything else," She pointed to the stuff from the basement that hadn't been thrown away by The Red Pen Theatre Troupe.

"A desk?"

"Not just a desk." Robyn bit the end of her pen. "All the furniture that was found in the basement. Just make it look nice, Travis. Rob, you'll have the toys and small things that look valuable, but don't seem to fit in any specific category."

"Okay," he said. "It's going to be great."

"What start time did you put on the signs?" Travis asked.

"Seven," Robyn answered and looked at her watch. "It's almost time."

"I think Grandma and Grandpa said they'd be come out closer to ten," I told Robyn. "But we could probably start without them."

"I'm guessing noon will be our busiest time," Travis said. "Considering the fact that many people go out for lunch on Sunday afternoons, they might see our signs and stop in for a bit."

"Do you think anyone is really going to buy shoes at a garage sale?" Audrey looked dissatisfied with her display.

"I bet," Carter said. "If we tell them it wasn't used. I mean, some still price tags on them."

"Too bad we can't just return them," Audrey sighed.

"C'mon Audrey," Rob took a seat on one of the plastic chairs we set out the night before. "It's going to be fun."

"Let's make it into a game," Robyn suggested. "Whoever can make the most money off their display wins."

"No fair," Travis shook his head. "No one is going to buy any of my stuff."

"Why would you say that?" I asked him. His display looked appealing enough.

"No one is coming to a garage sale to buy furniture," Travis laughed. "All I've got is a desk and three antique dining room chairs!"

"That's true, but most of your stuff costs like at least a hundred dollars," Robyn said.

"My chances are just lower, that's all," Travis said.

"Shh!" Robyn shrieked.

A bright red van rumbled down the street and slowed to a stop in front of Ms. Griffin's yard.

A young woman hopped out of the driver's side and waved. No one waved back. We were all too anxious to see what would happen next. She walked around the car and opened the van's side door. Three little boys in red and blue soccer uniforms raced out of the cars. They looked younger than Carter, but older than Lexie and Joshy.

"I knew it! Soccer moms!" Robyn cheered.

The lady walked closer and took a moment to look at my books first.

"Is there anything you're looking for in particular?" I asked her politely. Her kids had run straight to Rob's toy collection and he had to hold up things that actually seemed valuable above his head to keep the boys from breaking anything.

"Oh, no, no," the lady smiled. "Just browsing."

I let her go on and look at Travis's set up of furniture. I wasn't going to try and persuade her to buy anything. This was just a friendly garage sale.

Travis didn't see it that way.

"You know," Travis said slyly to the woman. "If you buy this desk, I'll help you move it for free."

"Aren't you a sweetheart," she smiled. "If I bought this desk, I'd doubt I'd need any help, though. I've got my own little movers." She tilted her head over to the little soccer boys who were still obsessed with the toys.

"They're so cute," Travis grinned.

"Yes, yes," The lady just sighed. "When we saw the signs at the intersection down the street, we just had to stop by. Might be a good distraction."

"Would you like any toys?" Rob asked.

"No, no," the lady laughed. "We've got enough at home."

"Then what is she doing here?" Carter murmured to me. "We want to be selling stuff, not just be a distraction."

"Be patient," I told him. "People usually buy stuff at garage sales for the cheap prices. I bet she'll find something that she'll like and want to buy it."

"We've got earrings and necklaces over here!" Audrey shouted. "All of this stuff has never been used."

"Never been used?" The lady looked confused and walked over to view some earrings. "How? This stuff is just lovely."

"The lady that lives here is a hoarder so we cleaned out her house this weekend and now we're selling things that she had bought but never used," Audrey said bluntly.

"Audrey!" Robyn snapped. "You shouldn't say that."

"No, no," the lady said. "It's alright, it's alright."

"Sorry," Audrey murmured. "I didn't mean to say anything awkward."

"Then just stop talking," Carter muttered under his breath.

"I'll take these." The lady pointed to a pair of pearly earrings. "I'll put those earrings to good use. Very good use."

"Told you she'd buy something," I poked Carter.

"You know," The lady paused after handing Robyn the money to pay. "I'm going to give you an extra three bucks. Just because you kids seem like you've been through a lot to get here."

"Wow, thanks!" Robyn smiled. The lady slipped the earring into her bag and snuck up behind the three boys.

"Let's go soccer stars." The young soccer mom picked up two of the three boys and nudged the third one with her foot.

She walked them all back to the car, buckled them all in, and drove off.

"Sympathy," Travis said. "She felt sorry for us."

"And that's good?" Robyn asked.

"No way," Travis said. "Audrey technically cheated at the game so I think I've won by default."

"You wish," Rob said. "Those kids were just dying to play with some of these toys. If anyone should win by default, it should be me."

"The game isn't over yet," Audrey said. "I still think that should count."

It was nice being with the other kids and not having any necessary supervision, but I missed my grandparents and Aunt Stella being around to help out.

At around seven-thirty, the crowds started to pour in. I had about six different people huddled around my two tables all the time and it was hard to keep up with all their questions. Most people wanted to pay me for the books they wanted, so I had to keep directing them over to Robyn who was collecting all the cash.

Grandma and Grandpa came out with Aunt Stella around ten after ten.

"How's everything going?" Grandma asked me as she walked over to my set up.

An older man was blowing his nose near my tables, so I didn't exactly hear her question.

"How's it going?" Grandma repeated.

"Pretty good," I smiled. "We seem to be getting a lot of business."

"Wow, that's wonderful," Grandma said. "Anyone who knows Ms. Griffin?"

"No, not yet," I said. "I kinda hope we don't see anyone who knows who lives here. It'd be difficult to explain."

"Well," Grandma looked past me. "I think I see someone right now."

"Huh?" I gasped and swung around.

"Howdy, little lady! Ian Kirchner at your service," Ian drove up the driveway and parked near the garage. His moustache shadow was shaved off, and it felt a little odd to see him without facial hair.

"Hi Ian!" I waved. "Do you want to buy some books?" I showed off my display.

"Looks good," He gave me a thumbs up. "But I'm mostly here to see your Aunt Stella."

"She's over there," Grandma pointed to Carter's silverware tables.

"Great, thanks a lot." Ian smiled a big, bright smile before heading off.

"Is the play still running?" I asked Grandma.

"I think that's what Ian is going to talk to Aunt Stella about," Grandma said. "He wants her to take the lead role permanently."

"Really?" I gasped. "That's awesome!"

"I know," Grandma grinned. "She's been working so hard too."

"How long is this little garage sale going to?" Grandpa asked as he hobbled over with a fork in his hand.

"Four o'clock is when Aunt Stella arranged for Father Brian to come back to take the tables to the church," Grandma told him. "Why do you have a fork?"

"Oh this?" Grandpa looked at his hand. "I brought it from home."

"Why?"

"I thought there was going to be food." Grandpa frowned. "Like a yogurt or something."

"Not at this garage sale," Grandma laughed. "The yard looks great, Grandpa. We did a great job with the flower beds."

I snuck away as they talked about the best kinds of soil to grow chrysanthemums.

"Hey Allison," Robyn said without looking up from her notes.

"Hi Robyn," I said back, peering over her shoulder to try and get a good look of how much money we'd raised so far.

"Stop doing that," She said, pushing my head back. "It's creepy."

"Sorry," I smirked. "How much money?"

"We're at five thousand five hundred," Robyn said.

"Dollars?" I gaped. "That's impossible."

"Oh, sorry," Robyn laughed. "I mean five hundred fifty dollars. I read that wrong."

"Well, that makes more sense," I said.

"It's more than I expected to make in the first three hours, sure," Robyn said. "But it's really not that much. Look at all this stuff!"

"I know, but we'll get there," I said. "How many dollars are you aiming to make?"

"At least three thousand," Robyn said. "That's about one-third of all the stuff we have set out."

"Gosh, that's a lot," I said. "But I bet we could do it."

"I know we can," Robyn boasted. "If only Travis could sell some of those great furniture pieces, we could get a thousand dollars easily."

"Just did," Travis walked up and handed Robyn a check for a thousand dollars. "I told the guy we were selling the antique desk for only three hundred dollars, but he insisted on paying a thousand dollars."

"Why?" I asked, a little bit suspicious. Usually people went to garage sales for the cheap prices.

"Said he was an antique dealer and felt bad if he bought it for just three hundred dollars," Travis said shrugging.

"Whoa," Robyn was speechless. "Did he say how much it was really worth?"

"Yeah," Travis frowned. "After he paid for it."

"This puts you in the lead, Travis," Robyn smiled. "Even if you were kinda swindled."

"At least he paid extra," I smirked and gave Travis a high five. "Nice job either way."

"Sweet!" Travis pumped his fist in the air. "I'm gonna win!"

"Not if I can help it!" Rob shouted as he approached the three of us. He had a stack of ones in his hand; most of them were crinkled and worn at the edges. "An old man just bought all his grandchildren Christmas presents!"

"It's summer!" I laughed.

"Yeah, weird right?" Rob grinned and handed Robyn the cash. "But I got one hundred dollars."

"That puts our total to one thousand six hundred fifty dollars," Robyn stuffed the cash and the check Travis had given her into her money folder and wrote the total on her notebook. "And it's not even noon!"

CHAPTER TWENTY-ONE

By the end of the garage sale, we had raised three thousand nine hundred ninety-eight dollars.

Robyn was overwhelmed with the success of the garage sale. When Father Brian came to pick up the tables and donations, we had barely anything to give him except a mismatched dish set, some old plaid shirts, and an ugly pair of purple curtains.

"Wow," Father Brian looked a little disappointed that there wasn't much to give to the needy. "Very impressive sales, children." He ruffled Carter's light blonde hair and shook Grandma's hand before leaving. "See you next Sunday!" He told her happily, before jumping back into his truck. The tables rattled in the back as he drove down the bumpy street.

"Here it is," Carter handed me the old, engraved watch. "I didn't want to forget about it again."

"Thanks," I smiled and stuck it in my pocket for safe-keeping.

The sky was still bright, only starting to turn purple, but everyone felt tired and wanted to go to sleep. Rob was slouched over in a yard chair, his hand over his eyes. Robyn and Audrey were half-asleep on the grass, picking dandelions.

"When will Ms. Griffin be back?" Grandma asked me. "I think the others are getting a little tired."

"They don't need to stick around," I said. "It's alright. I'll wait for her."

"Okay, I'll walk them home," Grandma said. "I'll call you when dinner is ready."

"Okay," I said and took a seat on the empty driveway.

I waited for a while alone, just thinking about the way I'd spent the last couple of days. I felt like we'd done a lot, but I knew that there would be more to come. Going through counseling would be hard for Ms. Griffin, and I wasn't going to be there once the summer ended to keep her morale up. I just prayed that all the work we'd done would be substantial enough to keep her going.

"Allison?" Aunt Stella took a seat next to me. "You've been out here for an hour."

It felt like only a second that I'd been alone, and I realized that this was one of the first moments all summer that I'd actually thought about what would happen if we'd failed.

"It's over," Aunt Stella smiled. "You can go back to being a kid."

"I guess so," I sighed. "But I'm not sure we're completely done."

"What do you mean?" Aunt Stella asked.

"Please promise me that you'll keep her company while I'm gone. I'm afraid that she'll start hoarding again."

"She won't," Aunt Stella said with a certain enthusiasm in her voice. "I know she won't."

"I believe you," I whispered, but I was still scared Ms. Griffin might lose sight of what was most important in her life. My doubts would have to wait to be proven, so I decided to change the subject. "I heard you got a main role in the play."

"How'd you hear about that?" Aunt Stella laughed. "But yes, it's true. Ian told me this morning."

"Congratulations," I smiled. "I guess all your hard work paid off."

"Like yours," She said, standing up. "I'm going inside, okay? Don't stay out here too long."

"I'm waiting for Ms. Griffin," I said.

"I know," she said and walked over the newly-trimmed yard back to our house.

I yawned and leaned back on the driveway. The shoes I'd thrown on that morning were squeezing my feet, and I could feel the blisters forming on the sides.

"Should have worn thicker socks," I sighed and closed my eyes.

My eyes were heavy and tired, and it felt like this was the first time they'd had a break all day. My breathing started to slow, and I began taking bigger breaths into my lungs. The thin wisps of hair that framed my face with curls tickled my ears as the summer wind started to blow harder.

"Allison?"

"Ah!" I jumped up with a start and scraped the bottom of my leg on the concrete.

"Whoa! Sorry, I didn't mean to wake you up." It was Jimmy.

"I was asleep?" I yawned, rubbing my eyes before standing to great him.

"How's everything?" He whispered to me.

"It's been pretty good, but there has definitely been a difference from the last time she was in her house." I grinned. "Is she in the car?"

"Yes," Jimmy said tilting his head over to the passenger side. The car was parked along the street and I could see Ms. Griffin's outline through the window. "Would it be alright if I brought her inside?"

"Of course!" I said.

"Did you ever find the watch?" Jimmy asked me. He looked less serious than the last time I saw him.

"Yep," I said reaching into my pockets. "It's right here." I pulled out the watch and handed it to him.

"Oh wow," He murmured as he studied the watch slowly. "I'm glad you found it."

"Actually, Carter found it," I said. "The others helped me a lot,"

"You can tell me all about it later," He said, walking back over to the car. "Do you want to come with us?"

"Well, I wouldn't want to intrude."

"She asked for you to come in with her," he said. "It'll be fine."

I waited by the house as Jimmy helped Ms. Griffin out of the car. Her face lit up when she saw her beloved house and she waved to me as she came closer.

"Allison!" Her smile was bright and her cheeks had a stronger hint of red than before. She gave me a hug and I could feel her heart beating fast.

"You shouldn't be scared," I told her. "Remember this is all for the best."

"I know," she said, but she didn't want to take another step closer. Her legs were stiff and her hands were shaking. Jimmy helped her up the stairs and I opened the front door.

"Basement first?" Jimmy suggested.

Ms. Griffin rocked back and forth and she began to cry. I'd never seen anyone so suddenly dazed and uncertain, and I started feeling bad about throwing out everything in her house.

But then I realized something. A smile was forming around her cheeks and her eyes weren't sad, but lively and sparkling. She looked me and whispered something so quiet I had to ask her to repeat what she'd said.

"I feel strange," her lips were barely moving. She clutched the old watch in her hands as she took her first step into the house.

There was a transformation taking place inside of her. Her facial expression conveyed a feeling of hesitation that I never saw before. All the stuff she'd used for her substitution for love was being replaced with something she'd missed for so long. The attachments to her things were less strong and her love for her family was multiplying like a virus.

"I can do this," Ms. Griffin's voice was hoarse, but the passion behind her words was overpowering. "I can."

CHAPTER TWENTY-TWO: EPILOGUE

The summer continued as normal from that point on. There were water battles, trampoline games, and treehouse adventures. Robyn and I decided not to tell the others the identity of the treehouse gift giver, and it became something we laughed about when the others tried to figure it out. Like any other summer, it was full of adventures. I kept visiting Ms. Griffin too; checking in on her, making sure she didn't start hoarding again and asking how her doctor visits were going. Jimmy said that it would be a long process, but that having friends and family to support her would make it easier. She continued getting help and spent many weekends with Jimmy and his family, just to have a reminder of who she was truly fighting for.

In the years that followed that crazy summer of stuff, I became a true friend of Ms. Griffin's. We became closer and had more to talk about each year. Jimmy would visit often, sometimes even with his kids. Carter, Audrey, Robyn, Travis, Rob and even Joshy and Lexie when they got a little older, visited Ms. Griffin's house frequently, exploring the garden or discovering new cookie baking techniques. She left her back door open for us and we came and went as if we were a part of her family. As we grew older, so did Ms. Griffin. We outgrew the treehouse around the same time that she couldn't climb the ladder anymore.

Ms. Griffin passed away on the Fifth of July the summer before my senior year of high school. Jimmy said she was happy when she passed, and that we shouldn't be sad that she'd died, but happy that she'd lived. He told me that she was smiling and that she was surrounded by family until the end. It was hard to hear, but I knew that the last years of her life were beautiful and full of love.

Months after Ms. Griffin's death, after our time at Grandma's house that summer, I received a letter in the mail. It was an official looking envelop from a law firm in the town where my Grandma lived. Inside was a typed note saying,

"Enclosed: Please find a letter to you left as part of the Griffin estate."

The letter was addressed from Ms. Griffin to me. For a moment, I thought that this was a sick joke from Carter or Audrey, but when I opened the letter, a little, rusted key fell from the package. The letter was in Ms. Griffin's own hand-writing and read in black ink.

Dear Allison,

Thank you for everything you have done and sacrificed for me. I have given you this key to show my appreciation. I hope you treasure this key until your next visit. This key opens the box in my shed that holds a special gift that I have given to you for your dedication to me. You have shown me that no amount of things will ever replace the part of your heart reserved for family. I hope you never forget your family and all they have done for you. Thank you, truly with all my heart.
Lots of love,
Beth Griffin

****

All year I kept that key near to me, never letting it leave my side. When I finally got back to my grandparent's house the next summer, the first thing I did was go to the shed. The house was now owned by Jimmy and his family. He wasn't ready to sell it. He wouldn't sell the house that had shaped so much of his life.

As I walked over to the shed, I smiled, remembering the first time I saw it; the day we were trying to figure out Eugene Griffin's obituary and the first time she made us cookies.

When I pushed open the shed door, the only thing left in there was a little wooden, locked box. I took the key that was around my neck and stuck it into the rusted opening. Inside was another note.

Allison, Thank you for changing my life. I hope this changes yours. –Beth Griffin

On top was the watch Carter had found so many years earlier. It had grown older too, but the broken face and worn gold only proved to me how important the watch really was to Ms. Griffin.

Underneath the watch was something I hadn't expected. I counted out slowly the stacks of fading, green twenty-dollar bills. I was stunned and felt horribly selfish. In total the money added up to be three thousand nine hundred ninety-eight dollars. It was all the money we made at the garage sale so many years earlier. I wished Ms. Griffin was there so I could've thanked her unmatched generosity. I wasn't going to put her money to waste. I would use it to change my life.

I felt like the only proper way to use that money was for my book, the novel that I would finally write. At that moment, I knew that my first book should be about that special summer, the summer of stuff.

ABOUT THE AUTHOR

Carolyn Bradley lives in Arlington, Virginia with her family. She is currently a student at Washington-Lee High School. Carolyn is an Army brat and has lived in Europe and many places across the United States. She uses her experiences to inspire her writing. *The Summer of Stuff* was originally drafted during the 2011 National Novel Writing Month (NaNoWriMo) program when she was twelve years old.

You can visit her at
www.carolynbradleybooks.com